20p

'THE BEST OF . . .'
collections are intended to present the
representative stories of the masters of
science fiction in chronological order, their
aim being to provide science fiction readers
with a selection of short stories that
demonstrate the authors' literary
development and at the same time provide
new readers with a sound introduction to
their work.

The collections were compiled with the
help and advice of the authors concerned,
together with the invaluable assistance of
numerous fans, without whose good work,
time and patience they would not have
been published.

In particular the advice of Roger Peyton,
Gerald Bishop, Peter Weston and Leslie
Flood is appreciated.

ANGUS WELLS, *Editor*, 1973

GW00686159

Also in this series and available from Sphere Books

THE BEST OF ISAAC ASIMOV 1939–49
THE BEST OF ISAAC ASIMOV 1954–72
THE BEST OF ARTHUR C. CLARKE 1937–55
THE BEST OF ARTHUR C. CLARKE 1956–72
THE BEST OF ROBERT HEINLEIN 1939–42
THE BEST OF FRANK HERBERT 1952–64
THE BEST OF FRANK HERBERT 1965–70
THE BEST OF FRITZ LEIBER
THE BEST OF CLIFFORD D. SIMAK
THE BEST OF A. E. VAN VOGT
THE BEST OF JOHN WYNDHAM 1932–49
THE BEST OF JOHN WYNDHAM 1951–1960

The Best of
Robert Heinlein
1947–1959

SPHERE BOOKS LIMITED
30/32 Gray's Inn Road, London WC1X 8JL

CONTENTS

Introduction 7

1947: The Green Hills of Earth 13

1949: The Long Watch 25

1950: The Man Who Sold the Moon 40

1959: All You Zombies 137

Bibliography 151

ACKNOWLEDGEMENTS

The Green Hills of Earth: *The Saturday Evening Post*, 1947
The Long Watch: *Shasta*, 1950
The Man Who Sold the Moon: *Shasta*, 1950
All You Zombies: *Fantasy & Science Fiction*, 1959

INTRODUCTION

NOT many readers of this book will remember the time when science fiction was considered pretty disreputable; so much so that no intelligent person was ever likely to admit that he actually read the stuff!

Fortunately some very clever people did read science fiction and their names have subsequently become more famous; Von Braun, Fred Hoyle, and others. Their efforts have helped to prove that science fiction was right all along, for we are now living in a futuristic world complete with atomic energy, moon landings, and many other wonders imagined by writers of thirty or forty years ago.

We can see it all in perspective now, but science fiction certainly was ridiculed in pre-war years and apparently with good reason. Ideas like space flight were thought silly, crackpot dreams then. Even as late as 1957 the Astronomer Royal could still state confidently that 'space travel is utter bilge'. That tends to show how sometimes even the experts cannot see beyond the ends of their noses.

Attitudes have changed in the last few decades, even though most of us didn't notice the changes taking place; and still don't. Most of us, that is, except for a small band of science-fiction writers who have helped to shape our future. Their job is to watch out for new marvels, and sometimes new dangers, before they actually arrive upon the scene. Of all these writers, Robert Heinlein stands out as the most influential.

From his very first story, 'Lifeline', he was examining new concepts at a giddying pace, including many which have since come true as well as others which are now very close upon the scientific horizon. For instance, not only did Heinlein predict atomic power in considerable detail before any such thing existed but he also wrote a remarkable story called 'Solution Unsatisfactory' which anticipated the ending of the then-current World War II through the use of atomic weapons. And further, he also predicted the subsequent nuclear stalemate between the United States and Soviet Union after the war – one wishes the politicians of the time had taken note!

Let's take another look at these achievements against the background of science fiction at the time Heinlein began writing. Although predictive fantasy is a very old literary tradition in the English language, the peculiarities of commercial publishing since 1926 had confined science fiction almost exclusively to the pages of a few American pulp magazines.

Despite the widespread acceptance of earlier pioneers such as Wells and contemporaries like Huxley (BRAVE NEW WORLD) science fiction was a pariah among literary *genres*, a field inhabited by indifferent writers practising erratic science in their fictional exploits.

Heinlein picked up science fiction and shook it until it rattled. He brought with him a background as an engineer and as a naval officer, and more important, he had a tremendous natural ability as a storyteller. Combining his fresh writing style with a disciplined understanding of modern technology, Heinlein was able to introduce an entirely new attitude to science fiction.

Almost for the first time in the specialist magazines, stories began to appear in which the Scientific Marvel was a beginning rather than an end in itself. Not surprisingly, other writers also began to lay more stress upon characterization and the treatment of human responses to new situations. Suddenly, science fiction took a large stride towards maturity.

In the three years 1939–42 Heinlein himself wrote twenty-eight stories, mostly for the leading mazagine, *Astounding*. This included three novels and a large part of his famous 'Future History', a bold attempt to build a consistent framework of events across a span of time from 1960–2600. Although the earliest items have now to some extent been overtaken by events they are still excellent reading, and four of these stories appear in this collection. They are 'The Roads Must Roll', 'The Green Hills of Earth', 'The Long Watch', and 'The Man Who Sold The Moon'.

'The Roads Must Roll' takes a concept popularized in Wells' WHEN THE SLEEPER WAKES, and shows how a system of moving pavements can replace the motor car when petroleum starts to be in short supply. According to Heinlein the first of these roadways would open in 1960, and it was a fair guess. It still might happen in a very similar way in the near future.

The mechanics of the system are fascinating, as the author shows how this new method of transport will revolutionize life in the same way as did the railways and motorways in their day. A closer reading reveals a lot more than that; the story is about people, the men who keep roadways rolling, and it demonstrates how organized labour can paralyse an industrial community. That theme, obviously, is as topical now as it ever was!

When the United States entered the last war Heinlein returned to research work, and did no further writing until 1946. He returned to science fiction, but his new stories were not submitted to the usual specialist magazines; quite correctly, he had judged that the broader reading public was ready for futuristic ideas, and the medium he chose was the prestige *Saturday Evening Post*.

It was unheard-of for such a magazine to publish science fiction, but the experience of V2 and Hiroshima were making people think. Heinlein found a ready market for the first of his post-war stories, 'The Green Hills of Earth'. This is a romantic tale of Rhysling, the blind singer who hung around the spaceways and whose songs of the solar system eventually pass into legend after his death.

'The Man Who Sold The Moon' was written a few years later and is particularly interesting. It was the final 'Future History' story although chronologically it is set at the very beginning of Heinlein's timescale. It returns to a character introduced in the 1940 story 'Requiem', and describes in detail how financier D. D. Harriman makes space travel possible.

The most obvious thing about the story is that it is completely wrong; it didn't happen that way. Apollo-11 has finally put to rest all those thousands of pre-1969 accounts of the first moon-landing, and this story is one of those peculiar literary animals, an *obsolete* piece of science fiction.

Heinlein describes how the Moon is conquered by a latter-day 'robber baron' of Free Enterprise America, kicking and fighting to build his rocket for mixed motives of greed and vision. Today we know that space is too big for that sort of thing, and we can see that moon rockets need the resources of a rich nation. We may even be tempted to think rather smugly that poor old Heinlein slipped up badly, back in 1950.

That's known as being wise after the event. Look instead at the matter-of-fact way in which Heinlein planned a believable expedition to the Moon at a time when orthodox scientists were so firmly convinced it could never be done. Besides getting his ballistics correct he also suggested a way of paying for the project, a doubly remarkable achievement because dreamers nearly always neglect to mention the cost of their visions!

Who knows, without the military-political 'space race', maybe the first moon landing could have happened in the way Heinlein had imagined, especially if some real-life figure like Rockefeller had stepped into Harriman's shoes.

Not that Heinlein ever intended his stories to be taken as literal prophecies in anything except the most general terms. His intentions were to try and show a future which was at least possible, and perhaps contained some of the things he would like to see as well as some he would rather avoid. 'The Long Watch' can certainly be taken as a warning, an illustration of the temptations of power in the same way as was shown in the more recent 'Dr Strangelove'.

Of the other tales presented here, 'Lifeline' remains a remarkably good first entry for any new writer to make into the professional field. It revolves around a process which in some way can look a little into the future and measure a person's lifespan – and tell him when he will die. Not surprisingly this proves a rather unpopular invention, and the author sketches in some of the results of owning such a device.

A similar 'gimmick' is invoked in 'And He Built A Crooked House', which is a fun story in its treatment of architecture. This one concerns a house built in the shape of an 'unfolded tesseract', (whatever that looks like!), and a convenient earthquake folds up the building and throws it into the fourth dimension.

This slightly whacky concept is a long way removed from

the much more thoughtful work Heinlein was turning out during the same period. As if to demonstrate his versatility even further, his last story before leaving for wartime duty was 'The Unpleasant Profession of Jonathan Hoag', which remains one of the few out-and-out fantasies he ever attempted.

The final story in this collection is also exceptional in its own way, for 'All You Zombies' is one of the only short stories written by Heinlein after 1953. For the last twenty years he has been almost exclusively a novelist; in that time he has written full-length books, many of which have aroused controversy with the science-fiction field, and four of which have won the coveted 'Hugo' Award.

The theme of this short, perfect 1959 story is time-travel, a subject which has fascinated Heinlein from 'Lifeline' onwards. Like his earlier 'By His Bootstraps' it deals with the sort of paradoxes which might result from travelling in time, and it wraps up these complications so well that nothing else remains to be said about the matter.

These eight stories show some of the many moods of Robert Heinlein, a master of descriptive, realistic narrative and unrivalled as an inventive thinker. Although science fiction generally dates so rapidly, far more quickly than other types of literature, it is quite remarkable to find the works in this book still read as fresh and original as when they first appeared.

This is the true measure of Heinlein. He should be judged not only for his skill as some sort of technological fortune-teller, but for his ability as a storyteller. Some of his science may be outdated in places but we can still thrill to the old magic of that scoundrel D. D. Harriman's first line, 'You've got to be a believer.' And then full-bent into the story! How I envy those of you who will discover Heinlein here, for the first time.

Peter R. Weston, 1973.

THE GREEN HILLS OF EARTH

THIS is the story of Rhysling, the Blind Singer of the Spaceways – but not the official version.

You sang his words in school:

> *I pray for one last landing*
> *On the globe that gave me birth;*
> *Let me rest my eyes on the fleecy skies*
> *And the cool, green hills of Earth.*

Or perhaps you sang in French, or German. Or it might have been Esperanto, while Terra's rainbow banner rippled over your head.

The language does not matter – it was certainly an *Earth* tongue. No one has ever translated *Green Hills* into the lisping Venerian speech; no Martian ever croaked and whispered it in the dry corridors. This is ours. We of Earth have exported everything from Hollywood crawlies to synthetic radioactives, but this belongs solely to Terra, and to her sons and daughters wherever they may be.

We have all heard many stories of Rhysling. You may even be one of the many who have sought degrees, or acclaim, by scholarly evaluations of his published works – *Songs of the Spaceways, The Grand Canal, and other Poems, High and Far,* and *Up Ship!*

Nevertheless, although you have sung his songs and read his verses, in school and out, your whole life, it is at least an even-money bet – unless you are a spaceman yourself – that you have never even heard of most of Rhysling's unpublished songs, such items as *Since the Pusher Met My Cousin, That Red-Headed Venusburg Gal, Keep Your Pants On, Skipper,* or *A Space Suit Built for Two.*

Nor can we quote them in a family magazine.

Rhysling's reputation was protected by a careful literary executor and by the happy chance that he was never interviewed. *Songs of the Spaceways* appeared the week he died; when it became a best seller, the publicity stories about him were pieced together from what people remembered about him plus the highly coloured handouts from his publishers.

The resulting traditional picture of Rhysling is about as authentic as George Washington's hatchet or King Alfred's cakes.

In truth you would not have wanted him in your parlour; he was not socially acceptable. He had a permanent case of sun itch, which he scratched continually, adding nothing to his negligible beauty.

Van der Voort's portrait of him for the Harriman Centennial edition of his works shows a figure of high tragedy, a solemn mouth, sightless eyes concealed by black silk bandage. He was never solemn! His mouth was always open, singing, grinning, drinking or eating. The bandage was any rag, usually dirty. After he lost his sight he became less and less neat about his person.

'Noisy' Rhysling was a jetman, second class, with eyes as good as yours, when he signed on for a loop trip to the Jovian asteroids in the RS *Goshawk*. The crew signed releases for everything in those days; a Lloyd's associate would have laughed in your face at the notion of insuring a spaceman. The Space Precautionary Act had never been heard of, and the Company was responsible only for wages, if and when. Half the ships that went farther than Luna City never came back. Spacemen did not care; by preference they signed for shares, and any one of them would have bet you that he could jump from the 200th floor of Harriman Tower and ground safely, if you offered him three to two and allowed him rubber heels for the landing.

Jetmen were the most carefree of the lot and the meanest. Compared with them the masters, the radarmen and the astrogators (there were no supers or stewards in those days) were gentle vegetarians. Jetmen knew too much. The others trusted the skill of the captain to get them down safely; jetmen knew that skill was useless against the blind and fitful devils chained inside their rocket motors.

The *Goshawk* was the first of Harriman's ships to be converted from chemical fuel to atomic power-piles – or rather the first that did not blow up. Rhysling knew her well; she was an old tub that had plied the Luna City run,

14

Supra-New York space station to Leyport and back, before she was converted for deep space. He had worked the Luna run in her and had been along on the first deep space trip, Drywater on Mars – and back, to everyone's surprise.

He should have made chief engineer by the time he signed for the Jovian loop trip, but, after the Drywater pioneer trip, he had been fired, blacklisted, and grounded at Luna City for having spent his time writing a chorus and several verses at a time when he should have been watching his gauges. The song was the infamous *The Skipper is a Father to his Crew*, with the uproariously unprintable final couplet.

The blacklist did not bother him. He won an accordion from a Chinese barkeep in Luna City by cheating at one-thumb and thereafter kept going by singing to the miners for drinks and tips until the rapid attrition in spacemen caused the Company agent there to give him another chance. He kept his nose clean on the Luna run for a year or two, got back into deep space, helped give Venusburg its original ripe reputation, strolled the banks of the Grand Canal when a second colony was established at the ancient Martial capital, and froze his toes and ears on the second trip to Titan.

Things moved fast in those days. Once the power-pile drive was accepted the number of ships that put out from the Luna-Terra system was limited only by the availability of crews. Jetmen were scarce; the shielding was cut to a minimum to save weight and few married men cared to risk possible exposure to radioactivity. Rhysling did not want to be a father, so jobs were always open to him during the golden days of the claiming boom. He crossed and re-crossed the system, singing the doggerel that boiled up in his head and chording it out on his accordion. The master of the *Goshawk* knew him; Captain Hicks had been astro-gator on Rhysling's first trip in her. 'Welcome home, Noisy.' Hicks had greeted him. 'Are you sober, or shall I sign the book for you?'

'You can't get drunk on the bug juice they sell here, Skipper.' He signed and went below, lugging his accordion.

Ten minutes later he was back. 'Captain,' he stated

darkly, 'that number two jet ain't fit. The cadmium dampers are warped.'

'Why tell me? Tell the Chief.'

'I did but he says they will do. He's wrong.'

The Captain gestured at the book. 'Scratch out your name and scram. We raise ship in thirty minutes.'

Rhysling looked at him, shrugged, and went below again.

It is a long climb to the Jovian planetoids; a Hawk-class clunker had to blast for three watches before going into free flight. Rhysling had the second watch. Damping was done by hand then, with the multiplying vernier and a danger gauge. When the gauge showed red, he tried to correct it – no luck.

Jetmen don't wait; that's why they are jetmen. He slapped the emergency discover and fished at the hot stuff with the tongs. The lights went out; he went right ahead. A jetman has to know his power room the way your tongue knows the inside of your mouth.

He sneaked a quick look over the top of the lead baffle when the lights went out. The blue radioactive glow did not help him any; he jerked his head back and went on fishing by touch.

When he was done he called over the tube, 'Number two jet out. And for crissake get me some light down here!'

There was light – the emergency circuit – but not for him. The blue radioactive glow was the last thing his optic nerve ever responded to.

As Time and Space come bending back to shape this star-specked scene,
The tranquil tears of tragic joy still spread their silver sheen;
Along the Grand Canal still soar the fragile Towers of Truth;
Their fairy grace defends this place of Beauty, calm and couth.
Bone-tired the race that raised the Towers, forgotten are their lores;
Long gone the gods who shed the tears that lap these crystal shores.

16

Slow beats the time-worn heart of Mars beneath this icy
sky;
The thin air whispers voicelessly that all who live must
die—

Yet still the lacy Spires of Truth sing Beauty's madrigal
And she herself will ever dwell along the Grand Canal!
—from *The Grand Canal,* by permission of
Lux Transcriptions, Ltd., London and Luna City

On the swing back they set Rhysling down on Mars at
Drywater; the boys passed the hat and the skipper kicked
in a half month's pay. That was all – *finis* – just another
space bum who had not got the good fortune to finish it off
when his luck ran out. He holed up with the prospectors
and archaeologists at How-Far? for a month or so, and
could probably have stayed for ever in exchange for his
songs and his accordion playing. But spacemen die if they
stay in one place; he hooked a crawler over to Drywater
again and thence to Marsopolis.

The capital was well into its boom; the processing plants
lined the Grand Canal on both sides and roiled the ancient
water with the filth of the run-off. This was before the Tri-
Planet Treaty forbade disturbing cultural relics for commerce; half the slender, fairylike towers had been torn
down, and others were disfigured to adapt them as pressurized buildings for Earthmen.

Now Rhysling had never seen any of these changes and
no one described them to him; when he 'saw' Marsopolis
again, he visualized it as it had been, before it was rational-
ized for trade. His memory was good. He stood on the
riparian esplanade where the ancient great of Mars had
taken their ease and saw its beauty spreading out before his
blinded eyes – ice blue plain of water unmoved by tide,
untouched by breeze and reflecting serenely the sharp,
bright stars of the Martial sky, and beyond the water the
lacy buttresses and flying towers of an architecture too
delicate for our rumbling, heavy planet.

The result was *Grand Canal.*

The subtle change in his orientation which enabled him to
see beauty at Marsopolis where beauty was not now began

17

to affect his whole life. All women became beautiful to him. He knew them by their voices and fitted their appearances to the sounds. It is a mean spirit indeed who will speak to a blind man other than in gentle friendliness; scolds who had given their husbands no peace sweetened their voices to Rhysling.

It populated his world with beautiful women and gracious men. *Dark Star Passing, Berenice's Hair, Death Song of a Wood's Colt*, and his other love songs of the wanderers, the womenless men of space, were the direct result of the fact that his conceptions were unsullied by tawdry truths. It mellowed his approach, changed his doggerel to verse, and sometimes even to poetry.

He had plenty of time to think now, time to get all the lovely words just so, and to worry a verse until it sang true in his head. The monotonous beat of *Jet Song*—

When the field is clear, the report all seen,
When the lock sighs shut, when the lights wink green,
When the check-off's done, when it's time to pray,
When the Captain nods, when she blasts away —
Hear the jets!
Hear them snarl at your back
When you're stretched on the rack;
Feel your ribs clamp your chest,
Feel your neck grind its rest.
Feel the pain in your ship,
Feel her strain in their grip.
Feel her rise! Feel her drive!
Straining steel, come alive,
On her jets!

—came to him not while he himself was a jetman but later while he was hitch-hiking from Mars to Venus and sitting out a watch with an old shipmate.

At Venusburg he sang his new songs and some of the old, in the bars. Someone would start a hat around for him; it would come back with the minstrel's usual take doubled or tripled in recognition of the gallant spirit behind the bandaged eyes.

It was an easy life. Any spaceport was his home and any ship his private carriage. No skipper cared to refuse to lift the extra mass of blind Rhysling and his squeeze box; he shuttled from Venusburg to Leyport to Drywater to New Shanghai or back again, as the whim took him.

He never went closer to Earth than Supra-New York Space Station. Even when signing the contract for *Songs of the Spaceways* he made his mark in a cabin-class liner somewhere between Luna City and Ganymede. Horowitz, the original publisher, was aboard for a second honeymoon and heard Rhysling sing at a ship's party. Horowitz knew a good thing for the publishing trade when he heard it; the entire contents of *Songs* were sung directly into the tape in the communications room of that ship before he let Rhysling out of his sight. The next three volumes were squeezed out of Rhysling at Venusburg, where Horowitz had sent an agent to keep him liquored up until he had sung all he could remember.

Up Ship! is not certainly authentic Rhysling throughout. Much of it is Rhysling's, no doubt, and *Jet Song* is unquestionably his, but most of the verses were collected after his death from people who had known him during his wanderings.

The Green Hills of Earth grew through twenty years. The earliest form we know about was composed before Rhysling was blinded, during a drinking bout with some of the indentured men on Venus. The verses were concerned mostly with the things the labour clients intended to do back on Earth if and when they ever managed to pay their bounties and thereby be allowed to go home. Some of the stanzas were vulgar, some were not, but the chorus was recognizably that of *Green Hills*.

We know exactly where the final form of *Green Hills* came from, and when.

There was a ship in at Venus Ellis Isle which was scheduled for the direct jump from there to Great Lakes, Illinois. She was the old *Falcon*, youngest of the Hawk class and the first ship to apply the Harriman Trust's new policy of extra-fare express service between Earth cities and any colony with scheduled stops. Rhysling decided to ride her back to Earth. Perhaps his own song had gotten under his skin – or perhaps he just hankered to see his native Ozarks one more time.

The Company no longer permitted deadheads; Rhysling knew this but it never occurred to him that the ruling might apply to him. He was getting old, for a spaceman, and just a little matter of fact about his privileges. Not senile – he simply knew that he was one of the landmarks in space, along with Halley's Comet, the Rings, and Brewster's Ridge. He walked in the crew's port, went below, and made himself at home in the first empty acceleration couch.

The Captain found him there while making a last-minute tour of his ship. 'What are you doing here?' he demanded.

'Dragging it back to Earth, Captain.' Rhysling needed no eyes to see a skipper's four stripes.

'You can't drag in this ship; you know the rules. Shake a leg and get out of here. We raise ship at once.' The Captain was young; he had come up after Rhysling's active time, but Rhysling knew the type – five years at Harriman Hall with only cadet practice trips instead of solid, deep space experience. The two men did not touch in background nor spirit; space was changing.

'Now, Captain, you wouldn't begrudge an old man a trip home.'

The officer hesitated – several of the crew had stopped to listen. 'I can't do it. "Space Precautionary Act, Clause Six: No one shall enter space save as a licensed member of a crew of a chartered vessel, or as a paying passenger of such a vessel under such regulations as may be issued pursuant to this act." Up you get and out you go.'

Rhysling lolled back, his hands under his head. 'If I've got to go, I'm damned if I'll walk. Carry me.'

The Captain bit his lip and said, 'Master-at-Arms! Have this man removed.'

The ship's policeman fixed his eyes on the overhead struts. 'Can't rightly do it, Captain. I've sprained my shoulder.' The other crew members, present a moment before, had faded into the bulkhead paint.

'Well, get a working party!'

'Aye, aye, sir.' He, too, went away.

Rhysling spoke again. 'Now look, Skipper – let's not have any hard feelings about this. You've got an out to carry me if you want to – the "Distressed Spaceman" clause.'

' "Distressed Spaceman", my eye! You're no distressed spaceman; you're a space-lawyer. I know who you are; you've been bumming around the system for years. Well, you won't do it in my ship. That clause was intended to succour men who had missed their ships, not to let a man drag free all over space.'

'Well, now, Captain, can you properly say I haven't missed my ship? I've never been back home since my last trip as a signed-on crew member. The law says I can have a trip back.'

'But that was years ago. You've used up your chance.'

'Have I now? The clause doesn't say a word about how soon a man has to take his trip back; it just says he's got it coming to him. Go look it up, Skipper. If I'm wrong, I'll not only walk out on my two legs, I'll beg your humble pardon in front of your crew. Go on – look it up. Be a sport.'

Rhysling could feel the man's glare, but he turned and stomped out of the compartment. Rhysling knew that he had used his blindness to place the Captain in an impossible position, but this did not embarrass Rhysling – he rather enjoyed it.

Ten minutes later the siren sounded, he heard the orders on the bull horn for Up-Stations. When the soft sighing of the locks and the slight pressure change in his ears let him know that take-off was imminent, he got up and shuffled down to the power room, as he wanted to be near the jets when they blasted off. He needed no one to guide him in any ship of the Hawk class.

Trouble started during the first watch. Rhysling had been lounging in the inspector's chair, fiddling with the keys of his accordion and trying out a new version of *Green Hills*.

> *Let me breathe unrationed air again*
> *Where there's no lack nor dearth*

And 'something, something, something "Earth"' – it would not come out right. He tried again.

> *Let the sweet fresh breezes heal me*
> *As they rove around the girth*
> *Of our lovely mother planet,*
> *Of the cool green hills of Earth.*

21

That was better, he thought. 'How do you like that, Archie?' he asked over the muted roar.

'Pretty good. Give out with the whole thing.' Archie Macdougal, Chief Jetman, was an old friend, both spaceside and in bars; he had been an apprentice under Rhysling many years and millions of miles back.

Rhysling obliged, then said, 'You youngsters have got it soft. Everything automatic. When I was twisting her tail you had to stay awake.'

'You still have to stay awake.' They fell to talking shop and Macdougal showed him the new direct response damping rig which had replaced the manual vernier control which Rhysling had used. Rhysling felt out the controls and asked questions until he was familiar with the new installation. It was his conceit that he was still a jetman and that his present occupation as a troubadour was simply an expedient during one of the fusses with the Company that any man could get into.

'I see you still have the old hand-damping plates installed,' he remarked, his agile fingers flitting over the equipment.

'All except the links. I unshipped them because they obscure the dials.'

'You ought to have them shipped. You might need them.'

'Oh, I don't know. I think —' Rhysling never did find out what Macdougal thought for it was at that moment the trouble tore loose. Macdougal caught it square, a blast of radioactivity that burned him down where he stood.

Rhysling sensed what had happened. Automatic reflexes of old habit came out. He slapped the discover and rang the alarm to the control room simultaneously. Then he remembered the unshipped links. He had to grope until he found them, while trying to keep as low as he could to get maximum benefit from the baffles. Nothing but the links bothered him as to location. The place was as light to him as any place could be; he knew every spot, every control, the way he knew the keys of his accordion.

'Power room! Power room! What's the alarm?'

'Stay out!' Rhysling shouted. 'The place is "hot".' He could feel it on his face and in his bones, like desert sunshine.

22

The links he got into place, after cursing someone, anyone, for having failed to rack the wrench he needed. Then he commenced trying to reduce the trouble by hand. It was a long job and ticklish. Presently he decided that the jet would have to be spilled, pile and all.

First he reported. 'Control!'

'Control aye aye!'

'Spilling jet three – emergency.'

'Is this Macdougal?'

'Macdougal is dead. This is Rhysling, on watch. Stand by to record.'

There was no answer; dumbfounded the Skipper may have been, but he could not interfere in a power room emergency. He had the ship to consider, and the passengers and crew. The doors had to stay closed.

The Captain must have been still more surprised at what Rhysling sent for record. It was:

> *We rot in the moulds of Venus,*
> *We retch at her tainted breath.*
> *Foul are her flooded jungles,*
> *Crawling with unclean death.*

Rhysling went on cataloguing the Solar System as he worked, '– harsh bright soil of Luna —', '– Saturn's rainbow rings —', '– the frozen night of Titan —', all the while opening and spilling the jet and fishing it clean. He finished with an alternate chorus —

> *We've tried each spinning space mote*
> *And reckoned its true worth:*
> *Take us back again to the homes of men*
> *On the cool, green hills of Earth.*

– then, almost absentmindedly remembered to tack on his revised first verse:

> *The arching sky is calling*
> *Spacemen back to their trade.*
> *All hands! Stand by! Free falling!*
> *And the lights below us fade.*

Out ride the sons of Terra,
Far drives the thundering jet,
Up leaps the race of Earthmen,
Out, far, and onward yet —

The ship was safe now and ready to limp home shy one jet. As for himself, Rhysling was not so sure. That 'sunburn' seemed pretty sharp, he thought. He was unable to see the bright, rosy fog in which he worked but he knew it was there. He went on with the business of flushing the air out through the outer valve, repeating it several times to permit the level of radioactivity to drop to something a man might stand under suitable armour. While he did this he sent one more chorus, the last bit of authentic Rhysling that ever could be :

We pray for one last landing
On the globe that gave us birth;
Let us rest our eyes on fleecy skies
And the cool, green hills of Earth.

THE LONG WATCH

Nine ships blasted off from Moon Base. Once in space, eight of them formed a globe around the smallest. They held this formation all the way to Earth.

The small ship displayed the insignia of an admiral – yet there was no living thing of any sort in her. She was not even a passenger ship, but a drone, a robot ship intended for radioactive cargo. This trip she carried nothing but a lead coffin – and a Geiger counter that was never quiet.

– from the editorial *After Ten Years*, film 38, 17 June 2009, Archives of the *N. Y. Times*

1

JOHNNY DAHLQUIST blew smoke at the Geiger counter. He grinned wryly and tried it again. His whole body was radioactive by now. Even his breath, the smoke from his cigarette, could make the Geiger counter scream.

How long had he been here? Time doesn't mean much on the Moon. Two days? Three? A week? He let his mind run back: the last clearly marked time in his mind was when the Executive Officer had sent for him, right after breakfast—

'Lieutenant Dahlquist, reporting to the Executive Officer.'

Colonel Towers looked up. 'Ah, John Ezra. Sit down, Johnny. Cigarette?'

Johnny sat down, mystified but flattered. He admired Colonel Towers, for his brilliance, his ability to dominate, and for his battle record. Johnny had no battle record; he had been commissioned on completing his doctor's degree in nuclear physics and was now junior bomb officer of Moon Base.

25

The Colonel wanted to talk politics; Johnny was puzzled. Finally Towers had come to the point; it was not safe (so he said) to leave control of the world in political hands; power must be held by a scientifically selected group. In short – the Patrol.

Johnny was startled rather than shocked. As an abstract idea, Towers's notion sounded plausible. The League of Nations had folded up; what would keep the United Nations from breaking up, too, and thus lead to another World War? 'And you know how bad such a war would be, Johnny.'

Johnny agreed. Towers said he was glad that Johnny got the point. The senior bomb officer could handle the work, but it was better to have both specialists.

Johnny sat up with a jerk. 'You are going to *do* something about it?' He had thought the Exec. was just talking.

Towers smiled. 'We're not politicians; we don't just talk. We act.'

Johnny whistled. 'When does this start?'

Towers flipped a switch. Johnny was startled to hear his own voice, then identified the recorded conversation as having taken place in the junior officers' messroom. A political argument he remembered, which he had walked out on ... a good thing, too! But being spied on annoyed him.

Towers switched it off. 'We *have* acted,' he said. 'We know who is safe and who isn't. Take Kelly —' He waved at the loudspeaker. 'Kelly is politically unreliable. You noticed he wasn't at breakfast?'

'Huh? I thought he was on watch.'

'Kelly's watch-standing days are over. Oh, relax; he isn't hurt.'

Johnny thought this over. 'Which list am I on?' he asked. 'Safe or unsafe?'

'Your name has a question mark after it. But I have said all along that you could be depended on.' He grinned engagingly. 'You won't make a liar of me, Johnny?'

Dahlquist didn't answer; Towers said sharply, 'Come now – what do you think of it? Speak up.'

'Well, if you ask me, you've bitten off more than you can chew. While it's true that Moon Base controls the Earth, Moon Base itself is a sitting duck for a ship. One bomb –

blooie!'

Towers picked up a message form and handed it over; it read: I HAVE YOUR CLEAN LAUNDRY – ZACK. 'That means every bomb in the *Trygve Lie* has been put out of commission. I have reports from every ship we need worry about.' He stood up. 'Think it over and see me after lunch. Major Morgan needs your help right away to change control frequencies on the bombs.'

'The control frequencies?'

'Naturally. We don't want the bombs jammed before they reach their targets.'

'What? You said the idea was to *prevent* war.'

Towers brushed it aside. 'There won't be a war – just a psychological demonstration, an unimportant town or two. A little blood-letting to save an all-out war. Simple arithmetic.'

He put a hand on Johnny's shoulder. 'You aren't squeamish, or you wouldn't be a bomb officer. Think of it as a surgical operation. And think of your family.'

Johnny Dahlquist had been thinking of his family. 'Please, sir, I want to see the Commanding Officer.'

Towers frowned. 'The Commodore is not available. As you know, I speak for him. See me again – after lunch.'

The Commodore was decidedly not available; the Commodore was dead. But Johnny did not know that.

Dahlquist walked back to the messroom, bought cigarettes, sat down, and had a smoke. He got up, crushed out the butt, and headed for the Base's west airlock. There he got into his spacesuit and went to the lockmaster. 'Open her up, Smitty.'

The marine looked surprised. 'Can't let anyone out on the surface without word from Colonel Towers, sir. Hadn't you heard?'

'Oh, yes! Give me your order book.' Dahlquist took it, wrote a pass for himself and signed it 'by direction of Colonel Towers'. He added, 'Better call the Executive Officer and check it.'

The lockmaster read it and stuck the book in his pocket. 'Oh, no, Lieutenant. Your word's good.'

'Hate to disturb the Executive Officer, eh? Don't blame

27

you.' He stepped in, closed the inner door, and waited for the air to be sucked out.

Out on the Moon's surface he blinked at the light and hurried to the track-rocket terminus; a car was waiting. He squeezed in, pulled down the hood, and punched the starting button. The rocket car flung itself at the hills, dived through and came out on a plain studded with projectile rockets, like candles on a cake. Quickly it dived into a second tunnel through more hills. There was a stomach-wrenching deceleration and the car stopped at the underground atom-bomb armoury.

As Dahlquist climbed out he switched on his walkie-talkie. The spacesuited guard at the entrance came to port-arms. Dahlquist said, 'Morning, Lopez,' and walked by him to the airlock. He pulled it open.

The guard motioned him back. 'Hey! Nobody goes in without the Executive Officer's say-so.' He shifted his gun, fumbled in his pouch and got out a paper. 'Read it, Lieutenant.'

Dahlquist waved it away. 'I drafted that order myself. *You* read it; You've misinterpreted it.'

'I don't see how, Lieutenant.'

Dahlquist snatched the paper, glanced at it, then pointed to a line. 'See? "– except persons specifically designated by the Executive Officer." That's the bomb officers, Major Morgan and me.'

The guard looked worried. Dahlquist said, 'Damn it, look up "specifically designated" – it's under "*Bomb Room, Security, Procedure for*," in your standing orders. Don't tell me you left them in the barracks!'

'Oh, no, sir! I've got 'em.' The guard reached into his pouch. Dahlquist gave him back the sheet; the guard took it, hesitated, then leaned his weapon against his hip, shifted the paper to his left hand, and dug into his pouch with his right.

Dahlquist grabbed the gun, shoved it between the guard's legs and jerked. He threw the weapon away and ducked into the airlock. As he slammed the door he saw the guard struggling to his feet and reaching for his side-arm. He dogged the outer door shut and felt a tingle in his fingers as a slug struck the door.

He flung himself at the inner door, jerked the spill lever, rushed back to the outer door, and hung his weight on the handle. At once he could feel it stir. The guard was lifting up; the lieutenant was pulling down, with only his low Moon weight to anchor him. Slowly the handle raised before his eyes.

Air from the bomb room rushed into the lock through the spill valve. Dahlquist felt his spacesuit settle on his body as the pressure in the lock began to equal the pressure in the suit. He quit straining and let the guard raise the handle. It did not matter; thirteen tons of air pressure now held the door closed.

He latched open the inner door to the bomb room, so that it could not swing shut. As long as it was open, the airlock could not operate; no one could enter.

Before him in the room, one for each projectile rocket, were the atom bombs, spaced in rows far enough apart to defeat any faint possibility of spontaneous chain reaction. They were the deadliest things in the known universe, but they were his babies. He had placed himself between them and anyone who would misuse them.

But, now that he was here, he had no plan to use his temporary advantage.

The speaker on the wall spluttered into life. 'Hey! Lieutenant! What goes on here? You gone crazy?' Dahlquist did not answer. Let Lopez stay confused — it would take him that much longer to make up his mind what to do. And Johnny Dahlquist needed as many minutes as he could squeeze. Lopez went on protesting. Finally he shut up.

Johnny had followed a blind urge not to let the bombs — *his* bombs! — be used for 'demonstrations on unimportant towns'. But what to do next? Well, Towers couldn't get through the lock. Johnny would sit tight until hell froze over.

Don't kid yourself, John Ezra! Towers could get in. Some high explosive against the outer door — then the air would whoosh out, our boy Johnny would drown in blood from his burst lungs — and the bombs would be sitting there, unhurt. They were built to stand the jump from Moon to Earth; vacuum would not hurt them at all.

He decided to stay in his spacesuit; explosive decompression didn't appeal to him. Come to think about it, death from old age was his choice.

Or they could drill a hole, let out the air, and open the door without wrecking the lock. Or Towers might even have a new airlock built outside the old. Not likely, Johnny thought; a *coup d'état* depended on speed. Towers was almost sure to take the quickest way – blasting. And Lopez was probably calling the Base right now. Fifteen minutes for Towers to suit up and get here, maybe a short dicker – then *whoosh*! the party is over.

Fifteen minutes —

In fifteen minutes the bombs might fall back into the hands of the conspirators; in fifteen minutes he must make the bombs unusable.

An atom bomb is just two or more pieces of fissionable metal, such as plutonium. Separated, they are no more explosive than a pound of butter; slapped together, they explode. The complications lie in the gadgets and circuits and gun used to slap them together in the exact way and at the exact time and place required.

These circuits, the bomb's 'brain', are easily destroyed – but the bomb itself is hard to destroy because of its very simplicity. Johnny decided to smash the 'brains' – and quickly!

The only tools at hand were simple ones used in handling the bombs. Aside from a Geiger counter, the speaker on the walkie-talkie circuit, a television rig to the base and the bombs themselves, the room was bare. A bomb to be worked on was taken elsewhere – not through fear of explosion, but to reduce radiation exposure for personnel. The radioactive material in a bomb is buried in a 'tamper' – in these bombs, gold. Gold stops alpha, beta, and much of the deadly gamma radiation – but not neutrons.

The slippery, poisonous neutrons which plutonium gives off had to escape, or a chain reaction – explosion! – would result. The room was bathed in an invisible, almost undetectable rain of neutrons. The place was unhealthy; regulations called for staying in it as short a time as possible.

The Geiger counter clicked off the 'background' radiation, cosmic rays, the trace of radioactivity in the Moon's crust, and secondary radioactivity set up all through the room by neutrons. Free neutrons have the nasty trait of infecting what they strike, making it radioactive, whether it be concrete wall or human body. In time the room would have to be abandoned.

Dahlquist twisted a knob on the Geiger counter, the instrument stopped clicking. He had used a suppressor circuit to cut out noise of 'background' radiation at the level then present. It reminded him uncomfortably of the danger of staying here. He took out the radiation exposure film all radiation personnel carry; it was a direct-response type and had been fresh when he arrived. The most sensitive end was faintly darkened already. Half-way down the film a red line crossed it. Theoretically, if the wearer was exposed to enough radioactivity in a week to darken the film to that line, he was, as Johnny reminded himself, a 'dead duck'.

Off came the cumbersome spacesuit; what he needed was speed. Do the job and surrender – better to be a prisoner than to linger in a place as 'hot' as this.

He grabbed a ball hammer from the tool rack and got busy, pausing only to switch off the television pick-up. The first bomb bothered him. He started to smash the cover plate of the 'brain,' then stopped, filled with reluctance. All his life he had prized fine apparatus.

He nerved himself and swung; glass tinkled, metal creaked. His mood changed; he began to feel a shameful pleasure in destruction. He pushed on with enthusiasm, swinging, smashing, destroying!

So intent was he that he did not hear his name called. 'Dahlquist! Answer me! Are you there?'

He wiped sweat and looked at the TV screen. Towers's perturbed features stared out.

Johnny was shocked to find that he had wrecked only six bombs. Was he going to be caught before he could finish? Oh, no! He *had* to finish. Stall, son, stall! 'Yes, Colonel? You called me?'

'I certainly did! What's the meaning of this?'

'I'm sorry, Colonel.'

Towers's expression relaxed a little. 'Turn on your pick-up, Johnny. I can't see you. What was that noise?'

'The pick-up is on,' Johnny lied. 'It must be out of order.

That noise – uh, to tell the truth, Colonel, I was fixing things so that nobody could get in here.'

Towers hesitated, then said firmly, 'I'm going to assume that you are sick and send you to the Medical Officer. But I want you to come out of there, right away. That's an order, Johnny.'

Johnny answered slowly, 'I can't just yet, Colonel. I came here to make up my mind and I haven't quite made it up. You said to see you after lunch.'

'I meant you to stay in your quarters.'

'Yes, sir. But I thought I ought to stand watch on the bombs, in case I decided you were wrong.'

'It's not for you to decide, Johnny. I'm your superior officer. You are sworn to obey me.'

'Yes, sir.' This was wasting time; the old fox might have a squad on the way now. 'But I swore to keep the peace, too. Could you come out here and talk it over with me? I don't want to do the wrong thing.'

Towers smiled. 'A good idea, Johnny. You wait there. I'm sure you'll see the light.' He switched off.

'There,' said Johnny, 'I hope you're convinced that I'm a half-wit – you slimy mistake!' He picked up the hammer, ready to use the minutes gained.

He stopped almost at once; it dawned on him that wrecking the 'brains' was not enough. There were no spare 'brains,' but there was a well-stocked electronics shop. Morgan could jury-rig control circuits for bombs. Why, he could himself – not a neat job, but one that would work. Damnation! He would have to wreck the bombs themselves – and in the next ten minutes.

But a bomb was solid chunks of metal, encased in a heavy tamper, all tied in with a big steel gun. It couldn't be done – not in ten minutes.

Damn!

Of course, there was one way. He knew the control circuits; he also knew how to beat them. Take this bomb; if he took out the safety bar, unhooked the proximity circuit, shorted the delay circuit and cut in the arming circuit by hand – then unscrewed *that* and reached in *there*, he could with just a long, stiff wire, set the bomb off.

Blowing the other bombs and the valley itself to Kingdom Come.

Also Johnny Dahlquist. That was the rub.

All this time he was doing what he had thought out, up to the step of actually setting off the bomb. Ready to go, the bomb seemed to threaten, as if crouching to spring. He stood up, sweating.

He wondered if he had the courage: he did not want to funk – and hoped that he had. He dug into his jacket and took out a picture of Edith and the baby. 'Honeychile,' he said, 'if I get out of this, I'll never even try to beat a red light.' He kissed the picture and put it back. There was nothing to do but wait.

What was keeping Towers? Johnny wanted to make sure that Towers was in blast range. What a joke on the jerk! Me – sitting here, ready to throw the switch on him. The idea tickled him; it led to a better: why blow himself up – alive?

There was another way to rig it – a 'dead man' control. Jigger up some way so that the last step, the one that set off the bomb, would not happen as long as he kept his hand on a switch or a lever or something. Then, if they blew open the door, or shot him, or anything – up goes the balloon!

Better still, if he could hold them off with the threat of it, sooner or later help would come – Johnny was sure that most of the Patrol was not in this stinking conspiracy – and then: Johnny comes marching home! What a reunion! He'd resign and get a teaching job; he'd stood his watch.

All the while he was working. Electrical? No, too little time. Make it a simple mechanical linkage. He had it doped out but had hardly begun to build it when the loudspeaker called him. 'Johnny?'

'That you, Colonel?' His hands kept busy.

'Let me in.'

'Well, now, Colonel, that wasn't in the agreement.' Where in blue blazes was something to use as a long lever?

'I'll come in alone, Johnny, I give you my word. We'll talk face to face.'

His word! 'We can talk over the speaker, Colonel.' Hey, that was it – a yardstick, hanging on the tool rack.

'Johnny, I'm warning you. Let me in, or I'll blow the door off.'

33

A wire – he needed a wire, fairly long and stiff. He tore the antenna from his suit. 'You wouldn't do that, Colonel. It would ruin the bombs.'

'Vacuum won't hurt the bombs. Quit stalling.'

'Better check with Major Morgan. Vacuum won't hurt them; explosive decompression would wreck every circuit.' The Colonel was not a bomb specialist; he shut up for several minutes. Johnny went on working.

'Dahlquist,' Towers resumed, 'that was a clumsy lie. I checked with Morgan. You have sixty seconds to get into your suit, if you aren't already. I'm going to blast the door.'

'No, you won't,' said Johnny. 'Ever heard of a "dead man" switch?' Now for a counterweight – and a sling.

'Eh? What do you mean?'

'I've rigged number seventeen to set off by hand. But I put in a gimmick. It won't blow while I hang on to a strap I've got in my hand. But if anything happens to me – *up she goes*! You are about fifty feet from the blast centre. Think it over.'

There was a short silence. 'I don't believe you.'

'No? Ask Morgan. He'll believe me. He can inspect it, over the TV pick-up.' Johnny lashed the belt of his space-suit to the end of the yardstick.

'You said the pick-up was out of order.'

'So I lied. This time I'll prove it. Have Morgan call me.'

Presently Major Morgan's face appeared. 'Lieutenant Dahlquist?'

'Hi, Stinky. Wait a sec.' With great care Dahlquist made one last connexion while holding down the end of the yardstick. Still careful, he shifted his grip to the belt, sat down on the floor, stretched an arm and switched on the TV pick-up. 'Can you see me, Stinky?'

'I can see you,' Morgan answered stiffly. 'What is this nonsense?'

'A little surprise I whipped up.' He explained it – what circuits he had cut out, what ones had been shorted, just how the jury-rigged mechanical sequence fitted in.

Morgan nodded. 'But you're bluffing, Dahlquist. I feel sure that you haven't disconnected the "K" circuit. You don't have the guts to blow yourself up.'

Johnny chuckled. 'I sure haven't. But that's the beauty of

34

it. It can't go off, *so long as I'm alive.* If your greasy boss, ex-Colonel Towers, blasts the door, then I'm dead and the bomb goes off. It won't matter to me, but it will to him. Better tell him.' He switched off.

Towers came on over the speaker shortly. 'Dahlquist?'

'I hear you.'

'There's no need to throw away your life. Come out and you will be retired on full pay. You can go home to your family. That's a promise.'

Johnny got mad. 'You keep my family out of this!'

'Think of them, man.'

'Shut up. Get back to your hole. I feel a need to scratch and this whole shebang might just explode in your lap.'

2

Johnny sat up with a start. He had dozed, his hand hadn't let go the sling, but he had the shakes when he thought about it.

Maybe he should disarm the bomb and depend on their not daring to dig him out? But Towers's neck was already in hock for treason; Towers might risk it. If he did and the bomb were disarmed, Johnny would be dead and Towers would have the bombs. No, he had gone this far; he wouldn't let his baby girl grow up in a dictatorship just to catch some sleep.

He heard the Geiger counter clicking and remembered having used the suppressor circuit. The radioactivity in the room must be increasing, perhaps from scattering the 'brain' circuits – the circuits were sure to be infected; they had lived too long too close to plutonium. He dug out his film.

The dark area was spreading towards the red line.

He put it back and said, 'Pal, better break this deadlock or you are going to shine like a watch dial.' It was a figure of speech; infected animal tissue does not glow – it simply dies, slowly.

The TV screen lit up; Towers's face appeared. 'Dahlquist? I want to talk to you.'

'Go fly a kite.'

'Let's admit you have us inconvenienced.'

'Inconvenienced, hell – I've got you stopped.'

'For the moment. I'm arranging to get more bombs —'

'Liar.'

'– but you are slowing us up. I have a proposition.'

'Not interested.'

'Wait. When this is over I will be chief of the world government. If you co-operate, even now, I will make you my administrative head.'

Johnny told him what to do with it. Towers said, 'Don't be stupid. What do you gain by dying?'

Johnny grunted. 'Towers, what a prime stinker you are. You spoke of my family. I'd rather see them dead than living under a two-bit Napoleon like you. Now go away – I've got some thinking to do.'

Towers switched off.

Johnny got out his film again. It seemed no darker but it reminded him forcibly that time was running out. He was hungry and thirsty – and he could not stay awake forever. It took four days to get a ship up from Earth; he could not expect rescue any sooner. And he wouldn't last four days – once the darkening spread past the red line he was a goner.

His only chance was to wreck the bombs beyond repair, and get out – before that film got much darker.

He thought about ways, then got busy. He hung a weight on the sling, tied a line to it. If Towers blasted the door, he hoped to jerk the rig loose before he died.

There was a simple, though arduous, way to wreck the bombs beyond any capacity of Moon Base to repair them. The heart of each was two hemispheres of plutonium, their flat surfaces polished smooth to permit perfect contact when slapped together. Anything less would prevent the chain reaction on which atomic explosion depended.

Johnny started taking apart one of the bombs.

He had to bash off four lugs, then break the glass envelope around the inner assembly. Aside from that the bomb came apart easily. At last he had in front of him two gleaming, mirror-perfect half globes.

A blow with the hammer – and one was no longer perfect. Another blow and the second cracked like glass; he had tapped its crystalline structure just right.

Hours later, dead tired, he went back to the armed bomb. Forcing himself to steady down, with extreme care he disarmed it. Shortly its silvery hemispheres too were useless. There was no longer a useable bomb in the room – but huge fortunes in the most valuable, most poisonous, and most deadly metal in the known world were spread around the floor.

Johnny looked at the deadly stuff. 'Into your suit and out of here, son,' he said aloud. 'I wonder what Towers will say?'

He walked towards the rack, intending to hang up the hammer. As he passed, the Geiger counter chattered wildly.

Plutonium hardly affects a Geiger counter; secondary infection from plutonium does. Johnny looked at the hammer, then held it closer to the Geiger counter. The counter screamed.

Johnny tossed it hastily away and started back towards his suit.

As he passed the counter it chattered again. He stopped short.

He pushed one hand close to the counter. Its clicking picked up to a steady roar. Without moving he reached into his pocket and took out his exposure film.

It was dead black from end to end.

3

Plutonium taken into the body moves quickly to bone marrow. Nothing can be done; the victim is finished. Neutrons from it smash through the body, ionizing tissue, transmuting atoms into radioactive isotopes, destroying and killing. The fatal dose is unbelievably small; a mass a tenth the size of a grain of table salt is more than enough – a dose small enough to enter through the tiniest scratch. During the historic 'Manhattan Project' immediate high amputation was considered the only possible first-aid measure.

Johnny knew all this but it no longer disturbed him. He sat on the floor, smoking a hoarded cigarette, and thinking. The events of his long watch were running through his mind.

He blew a puff of smoke at the Geiger counter and smiled without humour to hear it chatter more loudly. By now even his breath was 'hot' – carbon-14, he supposed, exhaled from his blood stream as carbon dioxide. It did not matter.

There was no longer any point in surrendering, nor would he give Towers the satisfaction – he would finish out this watch right here. Besides, by keeping up the bluff that one bomb was ready to blow, he could stop them from capturing the raw material from which bombs were made. That might be important in the long run.

He accepted, without surprise, the fact that he was not unhappy. There was a sweetness about having no further worries of any sort. He did not hurt, he was not uncomfortable, he was no longer even hungry. Physically he still felt fine and his mind was at peace. He was dead – he knew that he was dead; yet for a time he was able to walk and breathe and see and feel.

He was not even lonesome. He was not alone; there were comrades with him – the boy with his finger in the dike, Colonel Bowie, too ill to move but insisting that he be carried across the line, the dying Captain of the *Chesapeake* still with deathless challenge on his lips, Rodger Young peering into the gloom. They gathered about him in the dusky bomb room.

And of course there was Edith. She was the only one he was aware of. Johnny wished that he could see her face more clearly. Was she angry? Or proud and happy?

Proud though unhappy – he could see her better now and even feel her hand. He held very still.

Presently his cigarette burned down to his fingers. He took a final puff, blew it at the Geiger counter, and put it out. It was his last. He gathered several butts and fashioned a roll-your-own with a bit of paper found in a pocket. He lit it carefully and settled back to wait for Edith to show up again. He was very happy.

He was still propped against the bomb case, the last of his salvaged cigarettes cold at his side, when the speaker called out again. 'Johnny? Hey, Johnny! Can you hear me? This is Kelly. It's all over. The *Lafayette* landed and

38

Towers blew his brains out. Johnny? *Answer me.*'

When they opened the outer door, the first man in carried a Geiger counter in front of him on the end of a long pole. He stopped at the threshold and backed out hastily. 'Hey, chief!' he called. 'Better get some handling equipment – uh, and a lead coffin, too.'

Four days it took the little ship and her escort to reach Earth. Four days while all of Earth's people awaited her arrival. For ninety-eight hours all commercial programmes were off television; instead there was an endless dirge – the Dead March *from* Saul, *the* Valhalla *theme,* Going Home, *the* Patrol's own Landing Orbit.

The nine ships landed at Chicago Port. A drone tractor removed the casket from the small ship; the ship was then refuelled and blasted off in an escape trajectory, thrown away into outer space, never again to be used for a lesser purpose.

The tractor progressed to the Illinois town where Lieutenant Dahlquist had been born, while the dirge continued. There it placed the casket on a pedestal, inside a barrier marking the distance of safe approach. Space marines, arms reversed and heads bowed, stood guard around it; the crowds stayed outside this circle. And still the dirge continued.

When enough time had passed, long, long after the heaped flowers had withered, the lead casket was enclosed in marble, just as you see it today.

THE MAN WHO SOLD THE MOON

1

'You've got to be a believer!'

George Strong snorted at his partner's declaration. 'Delos, why don't you give up? You've been singing this tune for years. Maybe some day men will get to the Moon, though I doubt it. In any case, you and I will never live to see it. The loss of the power satellite washes the matter up for our generation.'

D. D. Harriman grunted. 'We won't see it if we sit on our fat behinds and don't do anything to make it happen. But we can make it happen.'

'Question number one: how? Question number two: why?'

'"Why?" The man asks "why". George, isn't there anything in your soul but discounts and dividends? Didn't you ever sit with a girl on a soft summer night and stare up at the Moon and wonder what was there?'

'Yeah, I did once. I caught a cold.'

Harriman asked the Almighty why he had been delivered into the hands of the Philistines. He then turned back to his partner. 'I could tell you why, the real "why", but you wouldn't understand me. You want to know why in terms of cash, don't you? You want to know how Harriman & Strong and Harriman Enterprises can show a profit, don't you?'

'Yes,' admitted Strong, 'and don't give me any guff about tourist trade and fabulous lunar jewels. I've had it.'

'You asked me to show figures on a brand-new type of enterprise, knowing I can't. It's like asking the Wright brothers at Kitty Hawk to estimate how much money Curtiss-Wright Corporation would some day make out of building airplanes. I'll put it another way. You didn't want us to go into plastic houses, did you? If you had had your way we would still be back in Kansas City, sub-dividing

40

cow-pastures and showing rentals.'

Strong shrugged.

'How much has New World Homes made to date?'

Strong looked absent-minded, while exercising the talent he brought to the partnership. 'Uh ... $172,946,004.62, after taxes, to the end of the last fiscal year. The running estimate to date is —'

'Never mind. What was our share in the take?'

'Well, uh, the partnership, exclusive of the piece you took personally and then sold to me later, has benefited from New World Homes during the same period by $13,010, 437.20, ahead of personal taxes. Delos, this double taxation has got to stop. Penalizing thrift is a sure way to run this country straight into —'

'Forget it, forget it! How much have we made of the Sky-blast Freight and Antipodes Transways?'

Strong told him.

'And yet I had to threaten you with bodily harm to get you to put up a dime to buy control of the injector patent. You said rockets were a passing fad.'

'We were lucky,' objected Strong. 'You had no way of knowing that there would be a big uranium strike in Australia. Without it, the Skyways group would have left us in the red. For that matter, New World Homes would have failed, too, if the road towns hadn't come along and given us a market out from under local building codes.'

'Nuts on both points. Fast transportation will pay; it always has. As for New World, when ten million families need new houses and we can sell 'em cheap, they'll buy. They won't let building codes stop them, not permanently. We gambled on a certainty. Think back, George: what ventures have we lost money on and what ones have paid off? Every one of my crack-brain ideas has made money, hasn't it? And the only time we've lost our ante was on conservative, blue-chip investments.'

'But we've made money on some conservative deals, too,' protested Strong.

'Not enough to pay for your yacht. Be fair about it, George; the Andes Development Company, the integrating pantograph patent, every one of my wildcat schemes I've had to drag you into – and every one of them paid.'

41

'I've had to sweat blood to make them pay,' Strong grumbled.

'That's why we are partners. I get a wildcat by the tail; you harness him and put him to work. Now we go to the Moon – and you'll make it pay.'

'Speak for yourself. I'm not going to the Moon.'

'I am.'

'Hummph! Delos, granting that we have got rich by speculating on your hunches, it's a steel-clad fact that if you keep on gambling you lose your shirt. There's an old saw about the pitcher that went once too often to the well.'

'Damn it, George – I'm going to the Moon! If you won't back me up, let's liquidate and I'll do it alone.'

Strong drummed on his desk-top. 'Now, Delos, nobody said anything about not backing you up.'

'Fish or cut bait. Now is the opportunity, and my mind's made up. I'm going to be the Man in the Moon.'

'Well ... let's get going. We'll be late to the meeting.'

As they left their joint office, Strong, always penny conscious, was careful to switch off the light. Harriman had seen him do so a thousand times; this time he commented. 'George, how about a light-switch that turns off automatically when you leave a room?'

'Hmm – but suppose someone were left in the room?'

'Well ... hitch it to stay on only when someone was *in* the room – key the switch to the human body's heat radiation, maybe.'

'Too expensive and too complicated.'

'Needn't be. I'll turn the idea over to Ferguson to fiddle with. It should be no larger than the present light-switch and cheap enough so that the power saved in a year will pay for it.'

'How would it work?' Strong asked.

'How should I know? I'm no engineer; that's for Ferguson and the other educated laddies.'

Strong objected. 'It's no good commercially. Switching off a light when you leave a room is a matter of temperament. I've got it; you haven't. If a man hasn't got it, you can't interest him in such a switch.'

'You can if power continues to be rationed. There is a

42

power shortage now; and there will be a bigger one.'

'Just temporary. This meeting will straighten it out.'

'George, there is nothing in this world so permanent as a temporary emergency. The switch will sell.'

Strong took out a notebook and stylus. 'I'll call Ferguson in about it tomorrow.'

Harriman forgot the matter, never to think of it again. They had reached the roof; he waved to a taxi, then turned to Strong. 'How much could we realize if we unloaded our holdings in Roadways and in Belt Transport Corporation – yes, and in New World Homes?'

'Huh? Have you gone crazy?'

'Probably. But I'm going to need all the cash you can shake loose for me. Roadways and Belt Transport are no good anyhow; we should have unloaded earlier.'

'You *are* crazy! It's the one really conservative venture you've sponsored.'

'But it wasn't conservative when I sponsored it. Believe me, George, road towns are on their way out. They are growing moribund, just as the railroads did. In a hundred years there won't be one left on the continent. What's the formula for making money, George?'

'Buy low and sell high.'

'That's only half of it ... *your* half. We've got to guess which way things are moving, give them a boost, and see that we are cut in on the ground floor. Liquidate that stuff, George; I'll need money to operate.'

The taxi landed; they got in and took off.

The taxi delivered them to the roof of the Hemisphere Power Building; they went to the power syndicate's board-room, as far below ground as the landing platform was above – in those days, despite years of peace, tycoons habitually came to rest at spots relatively immune to atom bombs. The room did not seem like a bomb shelter; it appeared to be a chamber in a luxurious penthouse, for a 'view window' back of the chairman's end of the table looked out high above the city, in convincing, live stereo, relayed from the roof.

The other directors were there before them. Dixon nodded as they came in, glanced at his watch finger and said, 'Well, gentlemen, our bad boy is here; we may as well

43

begin.' He took the chairman's seat and rapped for order.

'The minutes of the last meeting are on your pads as usual. Signal when ready.' Harriman glanced at the summary before him and at once flipped a switch on the table-top; a small green light flashed on at his place. Most of the directors did the same.

'Who's holding up the procession?' inquired Harriman, looking around. 'Oh – you, George. Get a move on.'

'I like to check the figures,' his partner answered testily, then flipped his own switch. A larger green light showed in front of Chairman Dixon, who then pressed a button; a transparency, sticking an inch or two above the table top in front of him, lit up with the word RECORDING.

'Operations report,' said Dixon and touched another switch. A female voice came out from nowhere. Harriman followed the report from the next sheet of paper at his place. Thirteen Curie-type power piles were now in operation, up five from the last meeting. The Susquehanna and Charleston piles had taken over the load previously borrowed from Atlantic Roadcity, and the roadways of that city were now up to normal speed. It was expected that the Chicago–Angeles road could be restored to speed during the next fortnight. Power would continue to be rationed, but the crisis was over.

All very interesting, but of no direct interest to Harriman. The power crisis that had been caused by the explosion of the power satellite was being satisfactorily met – very good, but Harriman's interest in it lay in the fact that the cause of inter-planetary travel had thereby received a setback from which it might not recover.

When the Harper–Erickson isotopic artificial fuels had been developed three years before it had seemed that, in addition to solving the dilemma of an impossibly dangerous power source which was also utterly necessary to the economic life of the continent, an easy means had been found to achieve interplanetary travel.

The Arizona power pile had been installed in one of the largest of the Antipodes rockets, the rocket powered with isotopic fuel created in the power pile itself, and the whole thing was placed in an orbit around the Earth. A much smaller rocket had shuttled between satellite and Earth, carrying supplies to the staff of the power pile, bringing back synthetic radioactive fuel for the power-hungry technology of Earth.

As a director of the power syndicate, Harriman had backed the power satellite – with a private axe to grind; he expected to power a Moon ship with fuel manufactured in the power satellite and thus to achieve the first trip to the Moon almost at once. He had not even attempted to stir the Department of Defence out of its sleep; he wanted no government subsidy – the job was a cinch; anybody could do it – and Harriman *would* do it. He had the ship; shortly he would have the fuel.

The ship had been a freighter of his own Antipodes line, her chem-fuel motors replaced, her wings removed. She still waited, ready for fuel – the recommissioned *Santa Maria*, née *City of Brisbane*.

But the fuel was slow in coming. Fuel had to be earmarked for the shuttle rocket; the power needs of a rationed continent came next – and those needs grew faster than the power satellite could turn out fuel. Far from being ready to supply him for a 'useless' Moon trip, the syndicate had seized on the safe but less efficient low-temperature uranium-salts and heavy water, Curie-type power piles as a means of using uranium directly to meet the ever-growing need for power, rather than build and launch more satellites.

Unfortunately the Curie piles did not provide the fierce star-interior conditions necessary for breeding the isotopic fuels needed for an atom-powered rocket. Harriman had reluctantly come around to the notion that he would have to use political pressure to squeeze the necessary priority for the fuels he wanted for the *Santa Maria*.

Then the power satellite had blown up.

Harriman was stirred out of his brown study by Dixon's voice. 'The operations report seems satisfactory, gentlemen. If there is no objection, it will be recorded as accepted. You will note that in the next ninety days we will be back up to the power level which existed before we were forced to close down the Arizona pile.'

'But with no provision for future needs,' pointed out

45

Harriman. 'There have been a lot of babies born while we have been sitting here.'

'Is that an objection to accepting the report, D. D.?'

'No.'

'Very well. Now the public relations report – let me call attention to the first item, gentlemen. The vice-president in charge recommends a schedule of annuities, benefits, scholarships, and so forth for dependants of the staff of the power satellite and of the pilot of the *Charon*: see Appendix "C".'

A director across from Harriman – Phineas Morgan, chairman of the food trust, Cuisine, Incorporated – protested, 'What is this, Ed? Too bad they were killed, of course, but we paid them sky-high wages and carried their insurance to boot. Why the charity?'

Harriman grunted. 'Pay it – I so move. It's peanuts. "Do not bind the mouths of the kine who tread the grain."'

'I wouldn't call better than nine hundred thousand "peanuts",' protested Morgan.

'Just a minute, gentlemen —' It was the vice-president in charge of public relations, himself a director. 'If you'll look at the breakdown, Mr Morgan, you will see that 85 per cent of the appropriation will be used to publicize the gifts.'

Morgan squinted at the figures. 'Oh – why didn't you say so? Well, I suppose the gifts can be considered unavoidable overheads, but it's a bad precedent.'

'Without them we have nothing to publicize.'

'Yes, but —'

Dixon rapped smartly. 'Mr Harriman has moved acceptance. Please signal your desires.' The tally board glowed green; even Morgan, after hesitation, okayed the allotment. 'We have a related item next,' said Dixon. 'A Mrs – uh, Garfield, through her attorneys, alleges that we are responsible for the congenital crippled condition of her fourth child. The putative facts are that her child was being born just as the satellite exploded and that Mrs Garfield was then on the meridian underneath the satellite, She wants the court to award her half a million.'

Morgan looked at Harriman. 'Delos, I suppose that *you* will say to settle it out of court.'

'Don't be silly. We fight it.'

Dixon looked around, surprised. 'Why, D. D.? It's my guess we could settle for ten or fifteen thousand – and that was what I was about to recommend. I'm surprised that the legal department referred it to publicity.'

'It's obvious why; it's loaded with high explosive. But we should fight, regardless of bad publicity. It's not like the last case; Mrs Garfield and her brat are not our people. And any dumb fool knows you can't mark a baby by radio-activity at birth; you have to get at the germ plasm of the previous generation at least. In the third place, if we let this get by, we'll be sued for every double-yolked egg that's laid from now on. This calls for an open allotment for defence and not one damned cent for compromise.'

'It might be very expensive,' observed Dixon.

'It'll be more expensive not to fight. If we have to, we should buy the judge.'

The public relations chief whispered to Dixon, then announced, 'I support Mr Harriman's view. That's my department's recommendation.'

It was approved. 'The next item,' Dixon went on, 'is a whole sheaf of suits arising out of slowing down the road cities to divert power during the crisis. They allege loss of business, loss of time, loss of this and that, but they all are based on the same issue. The most touchy, perhaps, is a stockholder's suit which claims that Roadways and this company are so interlocked that the decision to divert the power was not done in the interests of the stockholders of Roadways. Delos, this is your pigeon; want to speak on it?'

'Forget it.'

'Why?'

'Those are shotgun suits. This Corporation is not responsible; I saw to it that Roadways volunteered to sell the power because I anticipated this. And the directorates don't interlock; not on paper, they don't. That's why dummies were born. Forget it – for every suit you've got there, Roadways has a dozen. We'll beat them.'

'What makes you so sure?'

'Well' – Harriman lounged back and hung a knee over the arm of his chair – 'a good many years ago I was a Western Union messenger boy. While waiting around the office I read everything I could lay hands on, including the contract on the back of the telegram forms. Remember those? They used to come in big pads of yellow paper; by writing a message on the face of the form you accepted the contract in the fine print on the back – only most people didn't realize that. Do you know what that contract obligated the company to do?'

'Send a telegram, I suppose.'

'It didn't promise a durn thing. The Company offered to *attempt* to deliver the message, by camel caravan or snailback, or some equally stream-lined method, if convenient, but in event of failure the Company was not responsible. I read that fine print until I knew it by heart. It was the loveliest piece of prose I had ever seen. Since then all my contracts have been worded on the same principle. Anybody who sues Roadways will find that Roadways can't be sued on the element of time, because time is not of the essence. In the event of complete non-performance – which hasn't happened yet – Roadways is financially responsible only for freight charges or the price of the personal transportation tickets. So forget it.'

Morgan sat up. 'D. D., suppose I decided to run up to my country place tonight, by the roadway, and there was a failure of some sort so that I didn't get there until tomorrow? You mean to say Roadways is not liable?'

Harriman grinned. 'Roadways is not liable even if you starve to death on the trip. Better use your copter.' He turned back to Dixon. 'I move that we stall these suits and let Roadways carry the ball for us.'

'The regular agenda being completed,' Dixon announced later, 'time is allotted for our colleague Mr Harriman, to speak on a subject of his own choosing. He has not listed a subject in advance, but we will listen until it is your pleasure to adjourn.'

Morgan looked sourly at Harriman. 'I move we adjourn.'

Harriman grinned. 'For two cents I'd second that and let you die of curiosity.' The motion failed for want of a second. Harriman stood up.

'Mr Chairman, friends' – he then looked at Morgan –

'and associates. As you know, I am interested in space travel.'

Dixon looked at him sharply. 'Not that again, Delos! If I weren't in the chair, I'd move to adjourn myself.'

'"That again,"' agreed Harriman. 'Now and forever. Hear me out. Three years ago, when we were crowded into moving the Arizona power-pile out into space, it looked as if we had a bonus in the shape of interplanetary travel. Some of you here joined with me in forming Spaceways, Incorporated, for experimentation, exploration – and exploitation.

'Space was conquered; rockets that could establish orbits around the globe could be modified to get to the Moon – and from there, anywhere! It was just a matter of doing it. The problems remaining were financial – and political.

'In fact, the real engineering problems of space travel have been solved since World War II. Conquering space has long been a matter of money and politics. But it did seem that the Harper–Erickson process, with its concomitant of a round-the-globe rocket and a practical economical rocket fuel, had at last made it a very present thing, so close indeed that I did not object when the early allotments of fuel from the satellite were earmarked for industrial power.'

He looked around. 'I shouldn't have kept quiet. I should have squawked and brought pressure and made a hairy nuisance of myself until you allotted fuel to get rid of me. For now we have missed our best chance. The satellite is gone; the source of fuel is gone. Even the shuttle rocket is gone. We are back where we were in 1950. Therefore —'

He paused again. 'Therefore – I propose that we build a space ship and send it to the Moon!'

Dixon broke the silence. 'Delos, have you come unzipped? You just said that it was no longer possible. Now you say to build one.'

'I didn't say it was impossible; I said we had missed our best chance. The time is over-ripe for space travel. This globe grows more crowded every day. In spite of technical advances the daily food intake on this planet is lower than it was thirty years ago – and we get forty-six new babies every minute, 65,000 every day, 25,000,000 every year. Our race is about to burst forth to the planets; if we've got the initiative God promised an oyster we will help it along!

'Yes, we missed our best chance – but the engineering details can be solved. The real question is who's going to foot the bill? That is why I address you gentlemen, for right here in this room is the financial capital of this planet.'

Morgan stood up. 'Mr Chairman, if all *company* business is finished, I ask to be excused.'

Dixon nodded. Harriman said, 'So long, Phineas. Don't let me keep you. Now, as I was saying, it's a money problem, and here is where the money is. I move we finance a trip to the Moon.'

The proposal produced no special excitement; these men knew Harriman. Presently Dixon said. 'Is there a second to D. D.'s proposal?'

'Just a minute, Mr Chairman—' It was Jack Entenza, president of Two-Continents Amusement Corporation. 'I want to ask Delos some questions.' He turned to Harriman. 'D. D., you know I strung along when you set up Spaceways. It seemed like a cheap venture and possibly profitable in educational and scientific values – I never did fall for space liners plying between planets; that's fantastic. I don't mind playing along with your dreams to a moderate extent, but how do you propose to get to the Moon? As you say, you are fresh out of fuel.'

Harriman was still grinning. 'Don't kid me, Jack. I know why you came along. You weren't interested in science; you've never contributed a dime to science. You expected a monopoly on pix and television for your chain. Well, you'll get 'em, if you stick with me – otherwise I'll sign up 'Recreations, Unlimited'; they'll pay just to have you in the eye.'

Entenza looked at him suspiciously. 'What will it cost me?'

'Your other shirt, your eye-teeth, and your wife's wedding ring – unless 'Recreations' will pay more.'

'Damn you, Delos, you're crookeder than a dog's hind leg.'

'From you, Jack, that's a compliment. We'll do business. Now as to how I'm going to get to the Moon, that's a silly question. There's not a man in here who can cope with anything more complicated in the way of machinery than a knife and fork. You can't tell a left-handed monkey-wrench from a reaction engine, yet you ask me for blue-prints of a space-ship.

'Well, I'll tell you how I'll get to the Moon. I'll hire the proper brain boys, give them everything they want, see to it that they have all the money they can use, sweet talk them into long hours – then stand back and watch them produce. I'll run it like the Manhattan Project – most of you remember the A-bomb job; shucks, some of you can remember the Mississippi Bubble. The chap that headed up the Manhattan Project didn't know a neutron from Uncle George – but he got results. They solved that trick *four ways*. That's why I'm not worried about fuel; we'll get a fuel. We'll get several fuels.'

Dixon said, 'Suppose it works? Seems to me you're asking us to bankrupt the company for an exploit with no real value, aside from pure science, and a one-shot entertainment exploitation. I'm not against you – I wouldn't mind putting in ten, fifteen thousand to support a worthy venture – but I can't see the thing as a business proposition.'

Harriman leaned on his finger-tips and stared down the long table. 'Ten or fifteen thousand gum drops! Dan, I mean to get into you for a couple of megabucks *at least* – and before we're through you'll be hollering for more stock. This is the greatest real estate venture since the Pope carved up the New World. Don't ask me what we'll make a profit on; I can't itemize the assets – but I can lump them. The assets are a planet – a *whole planet*, Dan, that's never been touched. And more planets beyond it. If we can't figure out ways to swindle a few fast bucks out of a sweet set-up like that, then you and I had better both go on relief. It's like having Manhattan Island offered to you for twenty-four dollars and a case of whisky.'

Dixon grunted. 'You make it sound like the chance of a lifetime.'

'Chance of a lifetime, nuts! This is the greatest chance in all history. It's raining soup; grab yourself a bucket.'

Next to Entenza sat Gaston P. Jones, director of Trans-America and half a dozen other banks, one of the richest men in the room. He carefully removed two inches of cigar ash, then said drily, 'Mr Harriman, I will sell you all of my interest in the Moon, present and future, for fifty cents.'

Harriman looked delighted. 'Sold!'

Entenza had been pulling at his lower lip and listening with a brooding expression on his face. Now he spoke up. 'Just a minute, Mr Jones – I'll give you a dollar for it.'

'Dollar fifty,' answered Harriman.

'Two dollars,' Entenza answered slowly.

'Five!'

They edged each other up. At ten dollars Entenza let Harriman have it and sat back, still looking thoughtful. Harriman looked happily around. 'Which one of you thieves is a lawyer?' he demanded. The remark was rhetorical; out of seventeen directors the normal percentage – eleven, to be exact – were lawyers. 'Hey, Tony,' he continued, 'draw me up an instrument right *now* that will tie down this transaction so that it couldn't be broken before the Throne of God. All of Mr Jones's interests, rights, title, natural interest, future interests, interests held directly or through ownership of stock, presently held or to be acquired, and so forth and so forth. Put lots of Latin in it. The idea is that every interest in the Moon that Mr Jones now has or may acquire is mine – for a ten spot, cash in hand paid.' Harriman slapped a bill down on the table. 'That right, Mr Jones?'

Jones smiled briefly. 'That's right, young fellow.' He pocketed the bill. 'I'll frame this for my grandchildren – to show them how easy it is to make money.' Entenza's eyes darted from Jones to Harriman.

'Good!' said Harriman. 'Gentlemen, Mr Jones has set a market price for one human being's interest in our satellite. With around three billion persons on this globe that sets a price on the Moon of thirty billion dollars.' He hauled out a wad of money. 'Any more suckers? I'm buying every share that's offered, ten bucks a copy.'

'I'll pay twenty!' Entenza rapped out.

Harriman looked at him sorrowfully. 'Jack – don't do that! We're on the same team. Let's take the shares together, at ten.'

Dixon pounded for order. 'Gentlemen, please conduct

such transactions after the meeting is adjourned. Is there a second to Mr Harriman's motion?'

Gaston Jones said, 'I owe it to Mr Harriman to second his motion, without prejudice. Let's get on with a vote.'

No one objected; the vote was taken. It went eleven to three against Harriman – Harriman, Strong, and Entenza for; all others against. Harriman popped up before anyone could move to adjourn and said, 'I expected that. My real purpose is this: since the Company is no longer interested in space travel, will it do me the courtesy of selling me what I may need of patents, processes, facilities, and so forth now held by the company but relating to space travel and not relating to the production of power on this planet? Our brief honeymoon with the power satellite built up a back-log; I want to use it. Nothing formal – just a vote that it is the policy of the Company to assist me in any way not inconsistent with the primary interests of the Company. How about it, gentlemen? It'll get me out of your hair.'

Jones studied his cigar again. 'I see no reason why we should not accommodate him, gentlemen ... and I speak as the perfect disinterested party.'

'I think we can do it, Delos,' agreed Dixon, 'only we won't sell you anything, we'll *lend* it to you. Then, if you happen to hit the jackpot, the Company still retains an interest. Has anyone any objection?' he said to the room at large.

There was none; the matter was recorded as Company policy and the meeting was adjourned. Harriman stopped to whisper with Entenza and, finally, to make an appointment.

Gaston Jones stood near the door, speaking privately with Chairman Dixon. He beckoned to Strong, Harriman's partner. 'George, may I ask a personal question?'

'I don't guarantee to answer. Go ahead.'

'You've always struck me as a level-headed man. Tell me – why do you string along with Harriman? Why, the man's mad as a hatter.'

Strong looked sheepish. 'I ought to deny that, he's my friend ... but I can't. But dawggone it! Every time Delos has a wild hunch it turns out to be the real thing. I hate to string along – it makes me nervous – but I've learned to trust his hunches rather than another man's sworn financial report.'

Jones cocked one brow. 'The Midas touch, eh?'

'You could call it that.'

'Well, remember what happened to King Midas – in the long run. Good day, gentlemen.'

Harriman had left Entenza; Strong joined him. Dixon stood staring at them, his face very thoughtful.

2

Harriman's home had been built at the time when everyone who could was decentralizing and going underground. Above ground there was a perfect little Cape Cod cottage – the clapboards of which concealed armour plate – and most delightful, skilfully landscaped grounds; below ground there was four or five times as much floorspace, immune to anything but a direct hit and possessing an independent air supply with reserves for one thousand hours. During the Crazy Years the conventional wall surrounding the grounds had been replaced by a wall which looked the same but which would stop anything short of a broaching tank – nor were the gates weak points; their gadgets were as personally loyal as a well-trained dog.

Despite its fortress-like character, the house was comfortable. It was also very expensive to keep up.

Harriman did not mind the expense; Charlotte liked the house, and it gave her something to do. When they were first married she had lived uncomplainingly in a cramped flat over a grocery store; if Charlotte now liked to play house in a castle, Harriman did not mind.

But he was again starting a shoe-string venture; the few thousand per month of ready cash represented by the household expenses might, at some point in the game, mean the difference between success and the sheriff's bailiffs. That night at dinner, after the servants fetched the coffee and port, he took up the matter.

'My dear, I've been wondering how you would like a few months in Florida.'

His wife stared at him. 'Florida? Delos, is your mind

54

wandering? Florida is unbearable at this time of the year.'

'Switzerland, then. Pick your own spot. Take a real vacation, as long as you like.'

'Delos, you are up to something.'

Harriman sighed. Being 'up to something' was the unnameable and unforgivable crime for which any American male could be indicted, tried, convicted, and sentenced in one breath. He wondered how things had got rigged so that the male half of the race must always behave to suit feminine rules and feminine logic, like a snotty-nosed schoolboy in front of a stern teacher.

'In a way, perhaps. We've both agreed that this house is a bit of a white elephant. I was thinking of closing it, possibly even of disposing of the land – it's worth more now than when we bought it. Then, when we get around to it, we could build something more modern and a little less like a bombproof.'

Mrs Harriman was temporarily diverted. 'Well, I *have* thought it might be nice to build another place, Delos – say a little chalet tucked away in the mountains; nothing ostentatious, not more than two servants, or three. But we won't close this place until it's built, Delos – after all, one must live somewhere.'

'I was not thinking of building right away,' he answered cautiously.

'Why not? We're not getting any younger, Delos; if we are to enjoy the good things of life we had better not make delays. You needn't worry about it; I'll manage everything.'

Harriman turned over in his mind the possibility of letting her build to keep her busy. If he earmarked the cash for her 'little chalet' she would live in a hotel nearby wherever she decided to build it – and he could sell this monstrosity they were sitting in. With the nearest road city now less than ten miles away, the land should bring more than Charlotte's new house would cost and he would be rid of the monthly drain on his pocket-book.

'Perhaps you are right,' he agreed. 'But suppose you do build at once; you won't be living here; you'll be supervising every detail of the new place. I say we should unload this place; it's eating its head off in taxes, upkeep, and running expenses.'

She shook her head. 'Utterly out of the question, Delos. This is my home.'

He ground out an almost unsmoked cigar. 'I'm sorry, Charlotte, but you can't have it both ways. If you build, you can't stay here. If you stay here, we'll close these below-ground catacombs, fire about a dozen of the parasites I keep stumbling over, and live in the cottage on the surface. I'm cutting expenses.'

'Discharge the servants? Delos, if you think that I will undertake to make a home for you without a proper staff, you can just —'

'Stop it.' He stood up and threw his napkin down. 'It doesn't take a squad of servants to make a home. When we were first married you had *no* servants – and you washed and ironed my shirts into the bargain. But we had a home then. This place is owned by that staff you speak of. Well, we're getting rid of them, all but the cook and a handyman.'

She did not seem to hear him. 'Delos! Sit down and behave yourself. Now what's all this about cutting expenses? Are you in some sort of trouble? Are you? Answer me!'

He sat down wearily and answered, 'Does a man have to be in trouble to want to cut out unnecessary expenses?'

'In your case, yes. Now what is it? Don't try to evade me.'

'Now see here, Charlotte. We agreed a long time ago that I would keep business matters in the office. As for the house, we simply don't need a house this size. It isn't as if we had a passel of kids to fill up—'

'*Oh!* Blaming me for *that* again!'

'Now see here, Charlotte,' he wearily began again. 'I never did blame you and I'm not blaming you now. All I ever did was suggest that we both see a doctor and find out what the trouble was we didn't have any kids. And for twenty years you've been making me pay for that one remark. But that's all over and done with now; I was simply making the point that two people don't fill up twenty-two rooms. I'll pay a reasonable price for a new house, if you want it, and give you an ample household allowance.' He started to say how much, then decided not to. 'Or you can close this place and live in the cottage above. It's just that we are going to quit squandering money – for a while.'

She grabbed the last phrase. ' "For a while." What's going on, Delos? What are *you* going to squander money on?' When he did not answer she went on. 'Very well, if you won't tell me, I'll call George. He will tell me.'

'Don't do that, Charlotte. I'm warning you. I'll —'

'You'll what!' She studied his face. 'I don't need to talk to George; I can tell by looking at you. You've got the same look on your face you had when you came home and told me that you had sunk all our money in those crazy rockets.'

'Charlotte, that's not fair. Skyways paid off. It's made us a mint of money.'

'That's beside the point. I know why you're acting so strangely; you've got that old trip-to-the-Moon madness again. Well, I won't stand for it, do you hear? I'll stop you; I don't have to put up with it. I'm going right down in the morning and see Mr Kamens and find out what has to be done to make you behave yourself.' The cords of her neck jerked as she spoke.

He waited, gathering his temper before going on. 'Charlotte, you have no real cause for complaint. No matter what happens to me, your future is taken care of.'

'Do you think I want to be a widow?'

He looked thoughtfully at her. 'I wonder.'

'Why – why, you heartless *beast*.' She stood up. 'We'll say no more about it; do you mind?' She left without waiting for an answer.

His 'man' was waiting for him when he got to his room. Jenkins got up hastily and started drawing Harriman's bath.

'Beat it,' Harriman grunted. 'I can undress myself.'

'You require nothing more tonight, sir?'

'Nothing. But don't go unless you feel like it. Sit down and pour yourself a drink. Ed, how long you been married?'

'Don't mind if I do.' The servant helped himself. 'Twenty-three years, come May, sir.'

'How's it been, if you don't mind me asking?'

'Not bad. Of course there have been times —'

'I know what you mean. Ed, if you weren't working for me, what would you be doing?'

'Well, the wife and I have talked many times of opening a little restaurant – nothing pretentious, but good. A place where a gentleman could enjoy a quiet meal of good food.'

'Stag, eh?'

'No, not entirely, sir – but there would be a parlour for gentlemen only. Not even waitresses. I'd tend that room myself.'

'Better look around for locations, Ed. You're practically in business.'

3

Strong entered their joint offices the next morning at a precise nine o'clock, as usual. He was startled to find Harriman there before him. For Harriman to fail to show up at all meant nothing; for him to beat the clerks in was significant.

Harriman was busy with a terrestrial globe and a book – the current Nautical Almanac, Strong observed. Harriman barely glanced up. 'Morning, George. Say, who've we got a line to in Brazil?'

'Why?'

'I need some trained seals who speak Portuguese, that's why. And some who speak Spanish, too. Not to mention three or four dozen scattered around in this country. I've come across something very, very interesting. Look here ... according to these tables the Moon only swings about twenty-eight, just short of twenty-nine degrees north and south of the equator.' He held a pencil against the globe and spun it. 'Like that. That suggest anything?'

'No. Except that you're getting pencil-marks on a sixty-dollar globe.'

'And you an old real estate operator! What does a man own when he buys a parcel of land?'

'That depends on the deed. Usually mineral rights and other subsurface rights are —'

'Never mind that. Suppose he buys the works, without splitting the rights: how far down does he own? How far up does he own?'

'Well, he owns a wedge down to the centre of the Earth. That was settled in the slant-drilling and off-set oil lease

58

cases. Theoretically he used to own the space above the land, too, out indefinitely; but that was modified by a series of cases after the commercial air-lines came in – and a good thing for us, too, or we would have to pay tolls every time one of our rockets took off for Australia.'

'No, no, no, George! You didn't read those cases right. Right of passage was established – but *ownership* of the space above the land remained unchanged. And even right of passage was not absolute; you can build a thousand-foot tower on your own land right where airplanes, or rockets, or whatever, have been in the habit of passing and the ships will thereafter have to go above it, with no kick back on you. Remember how we had to lease the air south of Hughes Field to ensure that our approach wasn't built up?'

Strong looked thoughtful. 'Yes, I see your point. The ancient principle of land ownership remains undisturbed – down to the centre of the Earth, up to infinity. But what of it? It's a purely theoretical matter. You're not planning to pay tolls to operate those spaceships you're always talking about, are you?' He grudged a smile at his own wit.

'Not on your tin-type. Another matter entirely. George – *who owns the Moon*?'

Strong's jaw dropped, literally. 'Delos, you're joking.'

'I am not. I'll ask you again : if basic law says that a man owns the wedge of sky above his farm out to infinity, *who owns the Moon*? Take a look at this globe and tell me.'

Strong looked. 'But it can't mean anything, Delos. Earth laws wouldn't apply to the Moon.'

'They apply here, and that's where I am worrying about it. The Moon stays constantly over a slice of Earth bounded by latitude twenty-nine north and the same distance south; if one man owned all that belt of Earth – it's roughly the tropical zone – then he'd own the Moon, too, wouldn't he? By all the theories of real property ownership that our courts pay any attention to. And, by direct derivation, according to the sort of logic that lawyers like, the various owners of that belt of land have title – good vendable title – to the Moon somehow lodged collectively in them. The fact that the distribution of the title is a little vague wouldn't bother a lawyer; they grow fat on just such distributed titles every time a will is probated.'

59

'It's fantastic!'

'George, when are you going to learn that "fantastic" is a notion that doesn't bother a lawyer?'

'You're not planning to try to buy the entire tropical zone – that's what you would have to do.'

'No,' Harriman said slowly, 'but it might not be a bad idea to buy right, title, and interest in the Moon, as it may appear, from each of the sovereign countries in that belt. If I thought I could keep it quiet and not run the market up, I might try it. You can buy a thing awful cheap from a man if he thinks it's worthless and wants to sell before you regain your senses.

'But that's not the plan,' he went on. 'George, I want corporations – local corporations – in every one of those countries. I want the legislatures of each of those countries to grant franchises to its local corporation for lunar exploration, exploitation, et cetera, and the right to claim lunar soil on behalf of the country – with fee simple, naturally, being handed on a silver platter to the patriotic corporation that thought up the idea. And I want all this done quietly, so that the bribes won't go too high. We'll own the corporations, of course, which is why I need a flock of trained seals. There is going to be one hell of a fight one of these days over who owns the Moon; I want the deck stacked so that we win no matter how the cards are dealt.'

'It will be ridiculously expensive, Delos. And you don't even know that you will ever get to the Moon, much less that it will be worth anything after you get there.'

'We'll get there! It'll be more expensive not to establish these claims. Anyhow, it need not be very expensive; the proper use of bribe money is a homeopathic art – you use it as a catalyst. Back in the middle of the last century four men went from California to Washington with $40,000; it was all they had. A few weeks later they were broke – but Congress had awarded them a billion dollars' worth of railroad right of way. The trick is not to run up the market.'

Strong shook his head. 'Your title wouldn't be any good, anyhow. The Moon doesn't stay in one place; it passes *over* owned land certainly – but so does a migrating goose.'

'And nobody has title to a migrating bird. I get your point – but the Moon *always* stays over that one belt. If you move a boulder in your garden, do you lose title to it? Is it still real estate? Do the title laws still stand? This is like that group of real estate cases involving wandering islands in the Mississippi, George – the land moved as the river cut new channels, *but somebody always owned it*. In this case I plan to see to it that we are the "somebody".'

Strong puckered his brow 'I seem to recall that some of those island-and-riparian cases were decided one way and some another.'

'We'll pick the decisions that suit us. That's why law- yers' wives have mink coats. Come on, George; let's get busy.'

'On what?'

'Raising the money.'

'Oh.' Strong looked relieved. 'I thought you were plan- ning to use *our* money.'

'I am. But it won't be nearly enough. We'll use our money for the senior financing to get things moving; in the meantime we've got to work out ways to keep the money rolling in.' He pressed a switch at his desk; the face of Saul Kamens, their legal chief of staff, sprang out at him. 'Hey, Saul, can you slide in for a pow-wow?'

'Whatever it is, just tell them "no",' answered the at- torney. 'I'll fix it.'

'Good. Now come on in – they're moving Hell and I've got an option on the first ten loads.'

Kamens showed up in his own good time. Some minutes later Harriman had explained his notion for claiming the Moon ahead of setting foot on it. 'Besides those dummy corporations,' he went on, 'we need an agency that can receive contributions without having to admit any financial interest on the part of the contributor – like the National Geographic Society.'

Kamens shook his head. 'You can't buy the National Geographic Society.'

'Damn it, who said we were going to? We'll set up our own.'

'That's what I started to say.'

'Good. As I see it, we need at least one tax-free, non- profit corporation headed up by the right people – we'll hang on to voting control, of course. We'll probably need more than one; we'll set them up as we need them. And we've got to have at least one new ordinary corporation, not tax-free – but it won't show a profit until we are ready. The idea is to let the non-profit corporations have all the prestige and all the publicity – and the other gets all of the profits, if and when. We swap assets around between corporations, always for perfectly valid reasons, so that the non-profit corporations pay the expenses as we go along. Come to think about it, we had better have at least two ordinary corporations, so that we can let one of them go through bankruptcy if we find it necessary to shake out the water. That's the general sketch. Get busy and fix it up so that it's legal, will you?'

Kamens said, 'You know, Delos, it would be a lot more honest if you did it at the point of a gun.'

'A lawyer talks to me of honesty! Never mind, Saul; I'm not actually going to cheat anyone —'

'Hmmph!'

'– and I'm just going to make a trip to the Moon. That's what everybody will be paying for; that's what they'll get. Now fix it up so that it's legal, that's a good boy.'

'I'm reminded of something the elder Vanderbilt's lawyer said to the old man under similar circumstances: "It's beautiful the way it is; why spoil it by making it legal?" Okeh, brother gonoph, I'll rig your trap. Anything else?'

'Sure. Stick around. You might have some ideas. George, ask Montgomery to come in, will you?' Montgomery, Harriman's publicity chief, had two virtues in his employer's eyes: he was personally loyal to Harriman, and, secondly, he was quite capable of planning a campaign to convince the public that Lady Godiva wore a *Caresse*-brand girdle during her famous ride ... or that Hercules attributed his strength to Crunchies for breakfast.

He arrived with a large portfolio under his arm. 'Glad you sent for me, Chief. Get a load of this —' He spread the folder open on Harriman's desk and began displaying sketches and layouts. 'Kinsky's work – is that boy hot!'

Harriman closed the portfolio. 'What outfit is it for?'

'Huh? New World Homes.'

'I don't want to see it; we're dumping New World Homes. Wait a minute – don't start to bawl. Have the boys

62

go through with it; I want the price kept up while we un-load. But open your ears to another matter.' He explained rapidly the new enterprise.

Presently Montgomery was nodding. 'When do we start and how much do we spend?'

'Right away, and spend what you need to. Don't get chicken about expenses; this is the biggest thing we've ever tackled.' Strong flinched; Harriman went on, 'Have insomnia over it tonight; see me tomorrow and we'll kick it around.'

'Wait a sec, Chief. How are you going to sew up all those franchises from the, uh – the Moon states, those countries the Moon passes over, while a big publicity campaign is going on about a trip to the Moon and how big a thing it is for everybody? Aren't you about to paint yourself into a corner?'

'Do I look stupid? We'll get the franchises *before* you hand out so much as a filler – *you'll* get 'em, you and Kamens. That's your first job.'

'Hmmm....' Montgomery chewed a thumb-nail. 'Well, all right – I can see some angles. How soon do we have to sew it up?'

'I give you six weeks. Otherwise just mail your resigna-tion in, written on the skin off your back.'

'I'll write it right now, if you'll help me by holding a mirror.'

'Damn it, Monty, I know you can't do it in six weeks. But make it fast; we can't take a cent in to keep the thing going until you sew up those franchises. If you dilly-dally we'll all starve – and we won't get to the Moon either.'

Strong said, 'D. D., why fiddle with these trick claims from a bunch of moth-eaten tropical countries? If you are dead set on going to the Moon, let's call Ferguson in and get on with the matter.'

'I like your direct approach, George,' Harriman said, frowning. 'Mmmm ... back about 1845 or '46 an eager-beaver American army officer captured California. You know what the State Department did?'

'No.'

'They made him hand it back. Seems he hadn't touched second base, or something. So they had to go to the trouble

63

of capturing it all over again a few months later. Now I don't want that to happen to us. It's not enough just to set foot on the Moon and claim it; we've got to validate that claim in terrestrial courts – or we're in for a peck of trouble. Eh, Saul?'

Kamens nodded. 'Remember what happened to Columbus.'

'Exactly. We aren't going to let ourselves be rooked the way Columbus was.'

Montgomery spat out some thumb-nail. 'But, Chief – you know damn well those banana-state claims won't be worth two cents after I do tie them up. Why not get a franchise right from the UN and settle the matter? I'd as lief tackle that as tackle two dozen cock-eyed legislatures. In fact, I've got an angle already – we work it through the Security Council and –'

'Keep working on that angle; we'll use it later. You don't appreciate the full mechanics of the scheme, Monty. Of course those claims are worth nothing – except nuisance value. But their nuisance value is all-important. Listen: we get to the Moon, or appear about to. Every one of those countries puts up a squawk; we goose them into it through the dummy corporations they have enfranchised. Where do they squawk? To the UN, of course. Now the big countries on this globe, the rich and important ones, are all in the northern temperate zone. They see what the claims are based on and they take a frenzied look at the globe. Sure enough, the Moon does not pass over a single one of them. The biggest country of all – Russia – doesn't own a spadeful of dirt south of twenty-nine north. So they reject all the claims.

'Or do they?' Harriman went on. 'The US baulks. *The Moon passes over Florida and the southern part of Texas.* Washington is in a tizzy. Should they back up the tropical countries and support the traditional theory of land title, or should they throw their weight to the idea that the Moon belongs to everyone? Or should the United States try to claim the whole thing, seeing as how it was Americans who actually got there first?

'At this point we creep out from under cover. It seems that the Moon ship was owned and the expenses paid by a non-profit corporation chartered by the UN itself —'

'Hold it,' interrupted Strong. 'I didn't know that the UN could create corporations?'

'You'll find it can,' his partner answered. 'How about it, Saul?' Kamens nodded. 'Anyway,' Harriman continued. 'I've already got the corporation. I had it set up several years ago. It can do most anything of an educational or scientific nature – and, brother, that covers a lot of ground! Back to the point – this corporation, this creature of the UN, asks its parent to declare the lunar colony autonomous territory, under the protection of the UN. We won't ask for outright membership at first because we want to keep it simple —'

'Simple, he calls it!' said Montgomery.

'Simple. This new colony will be a *de facto* sovereign state, holding title to the entire Moon, and – listen closely! – capable of buying, selling, passing laws, issuing title to land, setting up monopolies, collecting tariffs, et cetera without end. *And we own it!*

'The reason we get all this is because the major states in the UN can't think up a claim that sounds as legal as the claim made by the tropical states, they can't agree among themselves as to how to split up the swag if they were to attempt brute force, and the other major states aren't willing to see the United States claim the whole thing. They'll take the easy way out of their dilemma by appearing to retain title in the UN itself. The real title, the title controlling all economic and legal matters, will revert to us. Now do you see my point, Monty?'

Montgomery grinned. 'Damned if I know if it's necessary, Chief, but I love it. It's beautiful.'

'Well, I don't think so.' Strong grumbled. 'Delos, I've seen you rig some complicated deals – some of them so devious that they turned even my stomach – but this one is the worst yet. I think you've been carried away by the pleasure you get out of cooking up involved deals in which somebody gets double-crossed.'

Harriman puffed hard on his cigar before answering, 'I don't give a damn, George. Call it chicanery, call it anything you want to. *I'm going to the Moon!* If I have to manipulate a million people to accomplish it, I'll do it.'

'But it's not necessary to do it this way.'

'Well, how would you do it?'

'Me? I'd set up a straightforward corporation. I'd get a resolution in Congress making my corporation the chosen instrument of the United States —'

'Bribery?'

'Not necessarily. Influence and pressure ought to be enough. Then I would set about raising the money and make the trip.'

'And the United States would then own the Moon?'

'Naturally,' Strong answered a little stiffly.

Harriman got up and began pacing. 'You don't see it, George, you don't see it. The Moon was not meant to be owned by a single country, even the United States.'

'It was meant to be owned by *you*, I suppose.'

'Well, if I own it – for a short while – I won't misuse it and I'll take care that others don't. Damnation, nationalism should stop at the stratosphere. Can you see what would happen if the United States lays claims to the Moon? The other nations won't recognize the claim. It will become a permanent bone of contention in the Security Council – just when we were beginning to get straightened out to the point where a man could do business planning, without having his elbow jogged by a war every few years. The other nations – quite rightfully – will be scared to death of the United States. They will be able to look up in the sky any night and see the main atom-bomb rocket base of the United States staring down the backs of their necks. Are they going to hold still for it? No, sirree – they are going to try to clip off a piece of the Moon for their own national use. The Moon is too big to hold, all at once. There will be other bases established there, and presently there will be the God-damnedest war this planet has ever seen – and we'll be to blame.

'No, it's got to be an arrangement that everybody will hold still for – and that's why we've got to plan it, think of all the angles, and be devious about it until we are in a position to make it work.

'Anyhow, George, if we claim it in the name of the United States, do you know where we will be, as business men?'

'In the driver's seat,' answered Strong.

'In a pig's eye! We'll be dealt right out of the game. The Department of National Defense will say, "Thank you, Mr Harriman. Thank you, Mr Strong. We are taking over in the interests of national security; you can go home now." And that's just what we would have to do – go home and wait for the next atom war.

'I'm not going to do it, George. I'm not going to let the brass hats muscle in. I'm going to set up a lunar colony and then nurse it along until it is big enough to stand on its own feet. I'm telling you – all of you! – this is the biggest thing for the human race since the discovery of fire. Handled right, it can mean a new and braver world. Handle it wrong and it's a one-way ticket to Armageddon. It's coming, it's coming soon whether we touch it or not. But I plan to be the Man in the Moon myself – and give it my personal attention to see that it's handled right.'

He paused. Strong said, 'Through with your sermon, Delos?'

'No, I'm not,' Harriman denied testily. 'You don't see this thing the right way. Do you know what we may find up there?' He swung his arm in an arc towards the ceiling. '*People!*'

'On the *Moon*?' said Kamens.

'Why not on the Moon?' whispered Montgomery to Strong.

'No, not on the Moon – at least I'd be amazed if we dug down and found anybody under that airless shell. The Moon has had its day; I was speaking of the other planets – Mars and Venus and the satellites of Jupiter. Even maybe out at the stars themselves. Suppose we do find people? Think what it will mean to us. We've been alone, all alone, the only intelligent race in the only world we know. We haven't even been able to talk with dogs or apes. Any answers we got we had to think up by ourselves, like deserted orphans. But suppose we find *people*, intelligent people, who have done some thinking in their own way. *We wouldn't be alone any more!* We could look up at the stars and never be afraid again.'

He finished, seeming a little tired, and even a little ashamed of his outburst, like a man surprised in a private

67

act. He stood facing them, searching their faces.

'Gee whiz, Chief,' said Montgomery, 'I can use that. How about it?'

'Think you can remember it?'

'Don't need to – I flipped on your "silent steno".'

'Well, damn your eyes!'

'We'll put it on video – in a play, I think.'

Harriman smiled almost boyishly. 'I've never acted, but if you think it'll do any good, I'm game.'

'Oh, no, not you, Chief.' Montgomery answered in horrified tones. 'You're not the type. I'll use Basil Wilkes-Booth, I think. With his organ-like voice and that beautiful archangel face he'll really send 'em.'

Harriman glanced down at his paunch and said gruffly, 'OK – back to business. Now about money. In the first place we can go after straight donations to one of the non-profit corporations, just like endowments for colleges. Hit the upper brackets, where tax deductions really matter. How much do you think we can raise that way?'

'Very little,' Strong opened. 'That cow is about milked dry.'

'It's never milked dry, as long as there are rich men around who would rather make gifts than pay taxes. How much will a man pay to have a crater on the Moon named after him?'

'I thought they all had names?' remarked the lawyer.

'Lots of them don't – and we have the whole back face that's not touched yet. We won't try to put down an estimate today; we'll just list it. Monty, I want an angle to squeeze dimes out of the school kids, too. Forty million school kids at a dime a head is $4,000,000.00 – we can use that.'

'Why stop at a dime?' asked Monty. 'If you get a kid really interested he'll scrape together a dollar.'

'Yes, but what do we offer him for it? Aside from the honour of taking part in a noble venture and so forth?'

'Mmmm....' Montgomery used up more thumb-nail. 'Suppose we go after both the dimes and the dollars. For a dime he gets a card saying that he's a member of the Moonbeam Club —'

'No, the "Junior Spacemen".'

'OK, the Moonbeams will be the girls – and don't forget to rope the Boy Scouts and the Girl Guides into it, too. We give each kid a card; when he kicks in another dime, we punch it. When he's punched out a dollar, we give him a certificate, suitable for framing, with his name and some process engraving, and on the back a picture of the Moon.'

'On the *front*,' answered Harriman. 'Do it in one print job; its cheaper and it'll look better. We give him something else, too, a steel-clad guarantee that his name will be on the rolls of the Junior Pioneers of the Moon, which same will be placed in a monument to be erected on the Moon at the landing-site of the first Moon-ship – in microfilm, of course; we have to watch weight.'

'Fine!' agreed Montgomery. 'Want to swap jobs, Chief? When he gets up to ten dollars we give him a genuine, solid gold-plated shooting-star pin, and he's a senior Pioneer, with the right to vote or something or other. And his name goes *outside* the monument – micro-engraved on a platinum strip.'

Strong looked as if he had bitten a lemon. 'What happens when he reaches a hundred dollars?' he asked.

'Why, then,' Montgomery answered happily, 'we give him another card and he can start over. Don't worry about it, Mr Strong – if any kid goes that high he'll have his reward. Probably we will take him on an inspection tour of the ship before it takes off and give him, absolutely free, a picture of himself standing in front of it, with the pilot's own signature signed across the bottom by some female clerk.'

'Chiselling from kids. Bah!'

'Not at all,' answered Montgomery in hurt tones. 'Intangibles are the most honest merchandise anyone can sell. They are always worth whatever you are willing to pay for them, and they never wear out. You can take them to your grave untarnished!'

'Hmmmph!'

Harriman listened to this, smiling and saying nothing.

Kamens cleared his throat. 'If you two ghouls are through cannibalizing the youth of the land, I've another idea.'

'Spill it.'

'George, you collect stamps, don't you?'

'Yes.'

'How much would a cover be worth which had been to the Moon and been cancelled there?'

'Huh? But you couldn't, you know.'

'I think we could get our Moon-ship declared a legal post office sub-station without too much trouble. What would it be worth?'

'Uh, that depends on how rare they are.'

'There must be some optimum number which will fetch a maximum return. Can you estimate it?'

Strong got a far-away look in his eye, then took out an old-fashioned pencil and commenced to figure. Harriman went on, 'Saul, my minor success in buying a share in the Moon from Jones went to my head. How about selling building lots on the Moon?'

'Let's keep this serious, Delos. You can't do that until you've landed there.'

'I am serious. I know you are thinking of that ruling back in the 'forties that such land would have to be staked out and accurately described. I want to sell land on the Moon, if I can – surface rights, mineral rights, anything.'

'Suppose they want to occupy it?'

'Fine. The more the merrier. I'd like to point out, too, that we'll be in a position to assess taxes on what we have sold. If they don't use it and won't pay taxes, it reverts to us. Now you figure out how to offer it, without going to jail. You may have to advertise it abroad, then plan to peddle it personally in this country, like Irish Sweepstake tickets.'

Kamens looked thoughtful. 'We could incorporate the land company in Panama and advertise by video and radio, from Mexico. Do you really think you can sell the stuff?'

'You can sell snowballs in Greenland,' put in Montgomery. 'It's a matter of promotion.'

Harriman added, 'Did you ever read about the Florida land boom, Saul? People bought lots they had never seen and sold them at tripled prices without ever having laid eyes on them. Sometimes a parcel would change hands a dozen times before anyone got around to finding out the stuff was ten-foot deep in water. We can offer bargains better than that: an acre, a guaranteed dry acre with plenty of sunshine, for maybe ten dollars – or a thousand acres at a dollar an acre. Who's going to turn down a bargain like that? Particularly after the rumour gets around that the Moon is believed to be loaded with uranium?'

'Is it?'

'How should I know? When the boom sags a little we will announce the selected location of Luna City – and it will just happen to work out that the land around the site is still available for sale. Don't worry, Saul; if it's real estate, George and I can sell it. Why, down in the Ozarks, where the land stands on edge, we used to sell both sides of the same acre.' Harriman looked thoughtful. 'I think we'll reserve mineral rights – there just might actually be uranium there!'

Kamens chuckled. 'Delos, you are a kid at heart. Just a great big, overgrown, lovable – juvenile delinquent.'

Strong straightened up. 'I make it half a million,' he said.

'Half a million what?' asked Harriman.

'For the cancelled philatelic covers, of course. That's what we were talking about. Five thousand is my best estimate of the number that could be placed with serious collectors and with dealers. Even then we will have to discount them to a syndicate and hold back until the ship is built and the trip looks like a probability.'

'Okay,' agreed Harriman. 'You handle it. I'll just note that we can tap you for an extra half-million towards the end.'

'Don't I get a commission?' asked Kamens. 'I thought of it.'

'You get a rising vote of thanks – and ten acres on the Moon. Now what other sources of revenue can we hit?'

'Don't you plan to sell stock?' asked Kamens.

'I was coming to that. Of course – but no preferred stock; we don't want to be forced through a reorganization. Participating common, non-voting —'

'Sounds like another banana-state corporation to me.'

'Naturally – but I want some of it on the New York Exchange, and you'll have to work that out with the Securities Exchange Commission somehow. Not too much of it – that's our showcase, and we'll have to keep it active and moving up.'

'Wouldn't you rather I swam the Hellespont?'

'Don't be like that, Saul. It beats chasing ambulances, doesn't it?'

'I'm not sure.'

'Well, that's what I want you – wups!' The screen on Harriman's desk had come to life. A girl said, 'Mr Harriman, Mr Dixon is here. He has no appointment, but he says that you want to see him.'

'I thought I had that thing shut off,' muttered Harriman, then pressed his key and said, 'OK, show him in.'

'Very well, sir – oh, Mr Harriman, Mr Entenza came in just this second.'

'Send them both in.' Harriman disconnected and turned back to his associates. 'Zip your lips, gang, and hold on to your wallets.'

'Look who's talking,' said Kamens.

Dixon came in with Entenza behind him. He sat down, looked around, started to speak, then checked himself.
He looked around again, especially at Entenza.

'Go ahead, Dan,' Harriman encouraged him. ' 'Tain't nobody here at all but just us chickens.'

Dixon made up his mind. 'I've decided to come in with you, D. D.,' he announced. 'As an act of faith I went to the trouble of getting this.' He took a formal-looking instrument from his pocket and displayed it. It was a sale of lunar rights, from Phineas Morgan to Dixon, phrased in exactly the same fashion as that which Jones had granted to Harriman.

Entenza looked startled, then dipped into his own inner coat pocket. Out came three more sales contracts of the same sort, each from a director of the power syndicate. Harriman cocked an eyebrow at them. 'Jack sees you and raises you two, Dan. You want to call?'

Dixon smiled ruefully. 'I can just see him.' He added two more to the pile, grinned, and offered his hand to Entenza.

'Looks like a stand off.' Harriman decided to say nothing just yet about seven telestated contracts now locked in his desk – after going to bed the night before he had been quite busy on the phone almost till midnight. 'Jack, how much did you pay for those things?'

'Standish held out for a thousand; the others were cheap.'

'Damn it, I warned you not to run the price up. Standish

72

will gossip. How about you, Dan?'

'I got them at satisfactory prices.'

'So you won't talk, eh? Never mind – gentlemen, how serious are you about this? How much money did you bring with you?'

Entenza looked to Dixon, who answered, 'How much does it take?'

'How much can you raise?' demanded Harriman.

Dixon shrugged. 'We're getting no place. Let's use figures. A hundred thousand.'

Harriman sniffed. 'I take it what you really want is to reserve a seat on the first regularly scheduled Moon ship. I'll sell it to you at that price.'

'Let's quit sparring, Delos. How much?'

Harriman's face remained calm, but he thought furiously. He was caught short, with too little information – he had not even talked figures with his Chief Engineer as yet. Confound it! Why had he left that phone hooked in? 'Dan, as I warned you, it will cost you at least a million just to sit down in this game.'

'So I thought. How much will it take to *stay* in the game?'

'All you've got.'

'Don't be silly, Delos. I've got more than you have.'

Harriman lit a cigar – his only sign of agitation. 'Suppose you match us, dollar for dollar.'

'For which I get two shares?'

'Okay, okay, you chuck in a buck whenever each of us does – share and share alike. But I run things.'

'You run the operations,' agreed Dixon. 'Very well, I'll put up a million now and match you as necessary. You have no objection to me having my own auditor, of course.'

'When have I ever cheated you, Dan?'

'Never, and there is no need to start.'

'Have it your own way – but be damned sure you send a man who can keep his mouth shut.'

'He'll keep quiet. I keep his heart in a jar in my safe.'

Harriman was thinking about the extent of Dixon's assets. 'We just might let you buy in with a second share later, Dan. This operation will be expensive.'

Dixon fitted his finger-tips carefully together. 'We'll meet that question when we come to it. I don't believe in letting

73

an enterprise fold up for lack of capital.'

'Good.' Harriman turned to Entenza. 'You heard what Dan had to say, Jack. Do you like the terms?'

Entenza's forehead was covered with sweat. 'I can't raise a million that fast.'

'That's all right, Jack. We don't need it this morning. Your note is good; you can take your time liquidating.'

'But you said a million is just the beginning. I can't match you indefinitely; you've got to place a limit on it. I've got my family to consider.'

'No annuities, Jack? No moneys transferred in an ir-revocable trust?'

'That's not the point. You'll be able to squeeze me – freeze me out.'

Harriman waited for Dixon to say something. Dixon finally said, 'We wouldn't squeeze you, Jack – as long as you could prove you had converted every asset you hold. We would let you stay in on a pro rata basis.'

Harriman nodded. 'That's right, Jack.' He was thinking that any shrinkage in Entenza's share would give himself and Strong a clear voting majority.

Strong had been thinking of something of the same nature, for he spoke up suddenly, 'I don't like this. Four equal partners – we can be deadlocked too easily.'

Dixon shrugged. 'I refuse to worry about it. I am in this because I am betting that Delos can manage to make it profitable.'

'We'll get to the Moon, Dan!'

'I didn't say that. I am betting that you will show a profit whether we get to the Moon or not. Yesterday evening I spent looking over the public records of several of your companies; they were very interesting. I suggest we resolve any possible deadlock by giving the Director – that's you, Delos – the power to settle ties. Satisfactory, Entenza?'

'Oh, sure!'

Harriman was worried, but tried not to show it. He did not trust Dixon, even bearing gifts. He stood up suddenly. 'I've got to run, gentlemen. I leave you to Mr Strong and Mr Kamens. Come along, Monty.' Kamens, he was sure, would not spill anything prematurely, even to nominal full partners. As for Strong – George, he knew, had not even let his left hand know how many fingers there were on his right.

He dismissed Montgomery outside the door of the partners' personal office and went across the hall. Andrew Ferguson, Chief Engineer of Harriman Enterprises, looked up as he came in.

'Howdy, Boss. Say, Mr Strong gave me an interesting idea for a light-switch this morning. It did not seem practical at first but—'

'Skip it. Let one of the boys have it and forget it. You know the line we are on now.'

'There have been rumours,' Ferguson answered cautiously.

'Fire the man that brought you the rumour. No – send him on a special mission to Tibet and keep him there until we are through. Well, let's get on with it. I want you to build a Moonship as quickly as possible.'

Ferguson threw one leg over the arm of his chair, took out a pen-knife, and began grooming his nails. 'You say that like it was an order to build a privy.'

'Why not? There have been theoretically adequate fuels since way back in '49. You get together the team to design it and the gang to build it; you build it – I pay the bills. What could be simpler?'

Ferguson stared at the ceiling. ' "Adequate fuels—" ' he repeated dreamily.

'So I said. The figures show that hydrogen and oxygen are enough to get a step rocket to the Moon and back – it's just a matter of proper design.'

' "Proper design," he says.' Ferguson went on in the same gentle voice, then suddenly swung around, jabbed the knife into the scarred desk-top and bellowed, 'What do you know about proper design? Where do I get the steels? What do I use for a throat liner? How in the hell do I burn enough tons of your crazy mix per second to keep from wasting all my power breaking loose? How can I get a decent mass-ratio with a step rocket? Why in the hell didn't you let me build a proper ship when we had the fuel?'

Harriman waited for him to quiet down, then said, 'What do we do about it, Andy?'

'Hmmm.... I was thinking about it as I lay abed last night – and my old lady is sore as hell at you; I had to finish the night on the couch. In the first place, Mr Harriman, the proper way to tackle this is to get a research appropriation from the Department of National Defense. Then you —'

'Damn it, Andy, you stick to engineering, and let me handle the political and financial side of it. I don't want your advice.'

'Damn it, Delos, don't go off half-cocked. This *is* engineering I'm talking about. The Government owns a whole mass of former art about rocketry – all classified. Without a government contract you can't even get a peek at it.'

'It can't amount to very much. What can a government rocket do that a Skyways rocket can't do? You told me yourself that Federal rocketry no longer amounted to anything.'

Ferguson looked supercilious. 'I am afraid I can't explain it in lay terms. You will have to take it for granted that we need those government research reports. There's no sense in spending thousands of dollars in doing work that has already been done.'

'Spend the thousands.'

'Maybe millions.'

'Spend the millions. Don't be afraid to spend money. Andy, I don't want this to be a military job.' He considered elaborating to the engineer the involved politics back of his decision, then thought better of it. 'How bad do you actually need that government stuff? Can't you get the same results by hiring engineers who used to work for the Government? Or even hire them away from the Government right now?'

Ferguson pursed his lips. 'If you insist on hampering me, how can you expect me to get results?'

'I am not hampering you. I am telling you that this is not a government project. If you won't attempt to cope with it on those terms, let me know now, so that I can find somebody who will.'

Ferguson started playing mumblety-peg on his desk top. When he got to 'noses' – and missed – he said quietly, 'I mind a boy who used to work for the Government at White

76

Sands. He was a very smart lad indeed – design chief of section.

'You mean he might head up your team?'

'That was the notion.'

'What's his name? Where is he? Who's he working for?'

'Well, as it happened, when the Government closed down White Sands, it seemed a shame to me that a good boy should be out of a job, so I placed him with Skyways. He's Maintenance Chief Engineer out on the Coast.'

'Maintenance? What a hell of a job for a creative man! But you mean he's working for us now? Get him on the screen. No – call the Coast and have them send him over here in a special rocket; we'll all have lunch together.'

'As it happens,' Ferguson said quietly. 'I got up last night and called him – that's what annoyed the Missus. He's waiting outside. Coster – Bob Coster.'

A slow grin spread over Harriman's face. 'Andy! You black-hearted old scoundrel, why did you pretend to baulk?'

'I wasn't pretending. I like it here, Mr Harriman. Just as long as you don't interfere, I'll do my job. Now my notion is this: we'll make young Coster Chief Engineer on the projects and give him his head. I won't joggle his elbow; I'll just read the reports. Then you leave him alone, d'you hear me? Nothing makes a good technical man angrier than to have some incompetent nitwit with a cheque-book telling him how to do his job.'

'Suits. And I don't want a penny-pinching old fool slowing him down, either. Mind you don't interfere with him, either, or I'll jerk the rug out from under you. Do we understand each other?'

'I think we do.'

'Then get him in here.'

Apparently Ferguson's concept of a 'lad' was about age thirty-five, for such Harriman judged Coster to be. He was tall, lean, and quietly eager. Harriman braced him immediately after shaking hands with, 'Bob, can you build a rocket that will go to the Moon?'

Coster took it without blinking. 'Do you have a source of X-fuel?' he countered, giving the rocket man's usual shorthand for the isotope fuel formerly produced by the power

77

satellite.

'No.'

Coster remained perfectly quiet for several seconds, then answered, 'I can put an unmanned messenger rocket on the face of the Moon.'

'Not good enough. I want it to go there, land, and come back. Whether it lands here under power or by atmosphere braking is unimportant.'

It appeared that Coster never answered promptly; Harriman had the fancy that he could hear wheels turning over in the man's head. 'That would be a very expensive job.'

'Who asked you how much it would cost? Can you do it?'

'I could try.'

'Try, hell. Do you think you can *do* it? Would you bet your shirt on it? Would you be willing to risk your neck in the attempt? If you don't believe in yourself, man, you'll always lose.'

'How much will *you* risk, sir? I told you this would be expensive – and I doubt if you have any idea how expensive.'

'And I told you not to worry about money. Spend what you need; it's my job to pay the bills. Can you do it?'

'I can do it. I'll let you know later how much it will cost and how long it will take.'

'Good. Start getting your team together. Where are we going to do this, Andy?' he added, turning to Ferguson. 'Australia?'

'No.' It was Coster who answered. 'It can't be Australia; I want a mountain catapult. That will save us one step-combination.'

'How big a mountain?' asked Harriman. 'Will Pikes Peak do?'

'It ought to be in the Andes,' objected Ferguson. 'The mountains are taller and closer to the equator. After all, we own facilities there – or the Andes Development Company does.'

'Do as you like, Bob,' Harriman told Coster. 'I would prefer Pikes Peak, but it's up to you.' He was thinking that there were tremendous business advantages to locating Earth's space-port #1 inside the United States – and he could visualize the advertising advantage of having Moon-ships blast off from the top of Pikes Peak, in plain view of everyone for hundreds of miles to the East.

'I'll let you know.'

'Now about salary. Forget whatever it was we were paying you; how much do you want?'

Coster actually gestured, waving the subject away. 'I'll work for coffee and cakes.'

'Don't be silly.'

'Let me finish. Coffee and cakes and one other thing: I got to make the trip.'

Harriman blinked. 'Well, I can understand that,' he said slowly, 'In the meantime I'll put you on a drawing account.' He added. 'Better calculate for a three-man ship, unless you are a pilot.'

'I'm not.'

'Three men, then. You see, I'm going along, too.'

4

'A good thing you decided to come in, Dan,' Harriman was saying, 'or you would find yourself out of a job. I'm going to put an awful crimp in the Power Company before I'm through with this.'

Dixon buttered a roll. 'Really? How?'

'We'll set up high-temperature piles, like the Arizona job, just like the one that blew up, around the corner on the far face of the Moon. We'll remote-control them; if one explodes it won't matter. And I'll breed more X-fuel in a week than the Company turned out in three months. Nothing personal about it; it's just that I want a source of fuel for interplanetary liners. If we can't get good stuff here, we'll have to make it on the Moon.'

'Interesting. But where do you propose to get the uranium for six piles? The last I heard the Atomic Energy Commission had the prospective supply earmarked twenty years ahead.'

'Uranium? Don't be silly; we'll get it on the Moon.'

'On the Moon? Is there uranium on the Moon?'

'Didn't you know? I thought that was why you decided to

join up with me?'

'No, I didn't know,' Dixon said deliberately. 'What proof have you?'

'Me? I'm no scientist, but it's a well-understood fact. Spectroscopy, or something. Catch one of the professors. But don't go showing too much interest; we aren't ready to show our hand.' Harriman stood up. 'I've got to run, or I'll miss the shuttle for Rotterdam. Thanks for the lunch.' He grabbed his hat and left.

Harriman stood up. 'Suit yourself, Mynheer van der Velde. I'm giving you and your colleagues a chance to hedge your bets. Your geologists all agree that diamonds result from volcanic action. What do you think we will find *there*?' He dropped a large photograph of the Moon on the Dutchman's desk.

The diamond merchant looked impassively at the pictured planet, pockmarked by a thousand giant craters. 'If you get there, Mr Harriman.'

Harriman swept up the picture. 'We'll get there. And we'll find diamonds – though I would be the first to admit that it may be twenty years or even forty before there is a big enough strike to matter. I've come to you because I believe that the worst villain in our social body is the man who introduces a major new economic factor without planning his innovation in such a way as to permit peaceful adjustment. I don't like panics. But all I can do is warn you. Good day.'

'Sit down, Mr Harriman. I'm always confused when a man explains how he is going to do *me* good. Suppose you tell me instead how this is going to do *you* good? Then we can discuss how to protect the world market against a sudden influx of diamonds from the Moon.'

Harriman sat down.

Harriman liked the Low Countries. He was delighted to discover a dog-drawn milk-cart whose young master wore real wooden shoes; he happily took pictures and tipped the child heavily, unaware that the set-up was arranged for tourists. He visited several other diamond merchants, but without speaking of the Moon. Among other purchases he found a brooch for Charlotte – a peace offering.

Then he took a taxi to London, planted a story with the representatives of the diamond syndicate there, arranged with his London solicitors to be insured by Lloyd's of London through a dummy, *against* a successful Moon flight, and called his home office. He listened to numerous reports, especially those concerning Montgomery, and found that Montgomery was in New Delhi. He called him there, spoke with him at length, then hurried to the port just in time to catch his ship. He was in Colorado the next morning.

At Peterson Field, east of Colorado Springs, he had trouble getting through the gate, even though it was now his domain, under lease. Of course he could have called Coster and got it straightened out at once, but he wanted to look around before seeing Coster. Fortunately the head guard knew him by sight; he got in and wandered around for an hour or more, a tri-coloured badge pinned to his coat to give him freedom.

The machine-shop was moderately busy, so was the foundry ... but most of the shops were almost deserted. Harriman left the shops, went into the main engineering building. The drafting-room and the loft were fairly active, as was the computation section. But there were unoccupied desks in the structures group and a churchlike quiet in the metals group and in the adjoining metallurgical laboratory. He was about to cross over into the chemicals and materials annexe when Coster suddenly showed up.

'Mr Harriman! I just heard you were here.'

'Spies everywhere,' remarked Harriman. 'I didn't want to disturb you.'

'Not at all. Let's go up to my office.'

Settled there a few moments later Harriman asked, 'Well – how's it going?'

Coster frowned. 'All right, I guess.'

Harriman noted that the engineer's desk baskets were piled high with papers which spilled over on to the desk. Before Harriman could answer, Coster's desk phone lit up and a feminine voice said sweetly, 'Mr Coster – Mr Morgenstern is calling.'

'Tell him I'm busy.'

After a short wait the girl answered in a troubled voice, 'He says he's just got to speak to you, sir.'

81

Coster looked annoyed. 'Excuse me a moment, Mr Harriman – OK, put him on.'

The girl was replaced by a man who said, 'Oh, there you are – what was the hold-up? Look, Chief, we're in a jam about these trucks. Every one of them that we leased needs an overhaul and now it turns out that the White Fleet Company won't do anything about it – they're sticking to the fine print in the contract. Now the way I see it, we'd do better to cancel the contract and do business with Peak City Transport. They have a scheme that looks good to me. They guarantee to —'

'Take care of it,' snapped Coster. 'You made the contract and you have authority to cancel. You know that.'

'Yes, but Chief, I figured this would be something you would want to pass on personally. It involves policy and —'

'Take care of it! I don't give a damn what you do as long as we have transportation when we need it.' He switched off.

'Who is that man?' inquired Harriman.

'Who? Oh, that's Morgenstern, Claude Morgenstern.'

'Not his name – what does he do?'

'He's one of my assistants – buildings, grounds, and transportation.'

'Fire him!'

Coster looked stubborn. Before he could answer a secretary came in and stood insistently at his elbow with a sheaf of papers. He frowned, initialled them, and sent her out.

'Oh, I don't mean that as an order,' Harriman added, 'but I do mean it as serious advice. I won't give orders in your backyard – but will you listen to a few minutes of advice?'

'Naturally,' Coster agreed stiffly.

'Mmm . . . this your first job as top boss?'

Coster hesitated, then admitted it.

'I hired you on Ferguson's belief that you were the engineer most likely to build a successful Moon-ship. I've had no reason to change my mind. But top administration ain't engineering, and maybe I can show you a few tricks there, if you'll let me.' He waited. 'I'm not criticizing,' he added, 'Top bossing is like sex; until you've had it, you don't know about it.' Harriman had the mental reservation that if the boy would not take advice, he would suddenly be out of a job, whether Ferguson liked it or not.

Coster drummed on his desk. 'I don't know what's wrong and that's a fact. It seems as if I can't turn anything over to anybody and have it done properly, I feel as if I were swimming in quicksand.'

'Done much engineering lately?'

'I try to.' Coster waved at another desk in the corner. 'I work there, late at night.'

'That's no good. I hired you as an engineer. Bob, this set-up is all wrong. This joint ought to be jumping – and it's not. Your office ought to be quiet as a grave. Instead your office is jumping and the plant looks like a graveyard.'

Coster buried his face in his hands, then looked up. 'I know it. I know what needs to be done – but every time I try to tackle a technical problem some bloody fool wants me to make a decision about trucks – or telephones – or some damn thing. I'm sorry, Mr Harriman. I thought I could do it.'

Harriman said very gently, 'Don't let it throw you, Bob. You haven't had much sleep lately, have you? Tell you what – we'll put over a fast one on Ferguson. I'll take that desk you're at for a few days and build you a set-up to protect you against such things. I want that brain of yours thinking about reaction vectors and fuel efficiencies and design stresses, not about contracts for trucks.' Harriman stepped to the door, looked around the outer office and spotted a man who might or might not be the office's chief clerk. 'Hey you! C'mere.'

The man looked startled, got up, came to the door, and said, 'Yes?'

'I want that desk in the corner and all the stuff that's on it moved to an empty office on this floor, right away.'

The clerk raised his eyebrows. 'And who are you, if I may ask?'

'God damn it —'

'Do as he tells you, Weber,' Coster put in.

'I want it down inside of twenty minutes,' added Harriman. 'Jump!'

He turned back to Coster's other desk, punched the phone, and presently was speaking to the main offices of

Skyways. 'Jim, is your boy Jock Berkeley around? Put him on leave and send him to me, at Peterson Field, right away, special trip. I want the ship he comes in to raise ground ten minutes after we sign off. Send his gear after him.' Harriman listened for a moment, then answered, 'No, your organization won't fall apart if you lose Jock – or, if it does, maybe we've been paying the wrong man the top salary ... okay, okay, you're entitled to one swift kick at my tail the next time you catch up with me, but send Jock. So long.'

He supervised getting Coster and his other desk moved into another office, saw to it that the phone in the new office was disconnected, and, as an afterthought, had a couch moved in there, too. 'We'll install a projector, and a drafting machine and bookcases and other junk like that tonight,' he told Coster. 'Just make a list of anything you need – to work on *engineering*. And call me if you want anything.' He went back to the nominal Chief Engineer's office and got happily to work trying to figure where the organization stood and what was wrong with it.

Some four hours later he took Berkeley in to meet Coster. The Chief Engineer was asleep at his desk, head cradled on his arms. Harriman started to back out, but Coster roused. 'Oh! Sorry,' he said, blushing. 'I must have dozed off.'

'That's why I brought you the couch,' said Harriman. 'It's more restful. Bob, meet Jock Berkeley. He's your new slave. You remain Chief Engineer and top, undisputed boss. Jock is Lord High Everything Else. From now on you've got absolutely nothing to worry about – except for the little detail of building a Moon-ship.'

They shook hands. 'Just one thing I ask, Mr Coster,' Berkeley said seriously. 'By-pass me all you want to – you'll have to run the technical show – but for God's sake record it so I'll know what's going on. I'm going to have a switch placed on your desk that will operate a sealed recorder at my desk.'

'Fine!' Coster was looking, Harriman thought, younger already.

'And if you want something that is not technical, don't do it yourself. Just flip a switch and whistle; it'll get done!' Berkeley glanced at Harriman. 'The Boss says he wants to talk with you about the real job, I'll leave you and get busy.' He left.

Harriman sat down; Coster followed suit and said, 'Whew!'

'Feel better?'

'I like the looks of that fellow Berkeley.'

'That's good; he's your twin brother from now on. Stop worrying; I've used him before. You'll think you're living in a well-run hospital. By the way, where do you live?'

'At a boarding-house, in the Springs.'

'That's ridiculous. And you don't even have a place here to sleep?' Harriman reached over to Coster's desk, got through to Berkeley. 'Jock – get a suite for Mr Coster at the Broadmoor, under a phoney name.'

'Right.'

'And have this stretch along here adjacent to his office fitted out as an apartment.'

'Right. Tonight.'

'Now, Bob, about the Moon-ship. Where do we stand?'

They spent the next two hours contentedly running over the details of the problem, as Coster had laid them out. Admittedly very little work had been done since the field was leased, but Coster had accomplished considerable theoretical work and computation before he had got swamped in administrative details. Harriman, though no engineer and certainly not a mathematician outside the primitive arithmetic of money, had for so long devoured everything he could find about space travel that he was able to follow most of what Coster showed him.

'I don't see anything here about your mountain catapult,' he said presently.

Coster looked vexed. 'Oh, that! Mr Harriman, I spoke too quickly.'

'Huh? How come? I've had Montgomery's boys drawing up beautiful pictures of what things will look like when we are running regular trips. I intend to make Colorado Springs the space-port capital of the world. We hold the franchise of the old cog railroad now; what's the hitch?'

'Well, it's both time and money.'

'Forget money. That's my pidgin.'

'Time, then. I still think an electric gun is the best way to get the initial acceleration for a chem-powered ship. Like this —' He began to sketch rapidly. 'It enables you to omit the first step-rocket stage, which is bigger than all the others put together and is terribly inefficient, as it has such a poor mass-ratio. But what do you have to do to get it? You can't build a tower, not a tower a couple of miles high, strong enough to take the thrusts – not this year, anyway. So you have to use a mountain. Pikes Peak is as good as any; it's accessible, at least.

'But what do you have to do to use it? First, a tunnel in through the side, from Manitou to just under the peak, and big enough to take the loaded ship —'

'Lower it down from the top,' suggested Harriman.

Coster answered, 'I thought of that. Elevators two miles high for loaded space-ships aren't exactly built out of string, in fact they aren't built out of any available materials. It's possible to gimmick the catapult itself so that the accelerating coils can be reversed and timed differently to do the job, but believe me, Mr Harriman, it will throw you into other engineering problems quite as great ... such as a giant railroad up to the top of the ship. And it still leaves you with the shaft of the catapult itself to be dug. It can't be as small as the ship, not like a gun-barrel for a bullet. It's got to be considerably larger; you don't compress a column of air two miles high with impunity. Oh, a mountain catapult could be built, but it might take ten years – or longer.'

'Then forget it. We'll build for the future, but not for this flight. No, wait – how about a *surface* catapult? We scoot up the side of the mountain and curve it up at the end?'

'Quite frankly, I think something like that is what will eventually be used. But, as of today, it just creates new problems. Even if we could devise an electric gun in which you could make that last curve – we can't at present – the ship would have to be designed for terrific side-stresses and all the additional weight would be parasitic so far as our main purpose is concerned, the design of a rocket ship.'

'Well, Bob, what *is* your solution?'

Coster frowned. 'Go back to what we know how to do – build a step rocket.'

'Monty —'

'Yeah, Chief?'

'Have you ever heard this song?' Harriman hummed, *The Moon belongs to everyone; the best things in life are free* —', then sang it, badly off key.

'Can't say as I ever have.'

'It was before your time. I want it dug out again. I want it revived, plugged until Hell wouldn't have it, and on everybody's lips.'

'OK.' Montgomery took out his memorandum pad. 'When do you want it to reach its top?'

Harriman considered. 'In, say, about three months. Then I want the first phrase picked up and used in advertising slogans.'

'A cinch.'

'How are things in Florida, Monty?'

'I thought we were going to have to buy the whole damned legislature until we got the rumour spread around that Los Angeles had contracted to have a City-Limits-of-Los-Angeles sign planted on the Moon for publicity pix. Then they came around.'

'Good.' Harriman pondered. 'You know, that's not a bad idea. How much do you think the Chamber of Commerce of Los Angeles would pay for such a picture?'

Montgomery made another note. 'I'll look into it.'

'I suppose you are about ready to crank up Texas, now that Florida is loaded?'

'Most any time. We're spreading a few side rumours first.'

Headline from Dallas–Fort Worth *Banner*:

'THE MOON BELONGS TO TEXAS! ! !'

'— and that's all for tonight, kiddies. Don't forget to send in those box tops, or reasonable facsimiles. Remember – first prize is a thousand-acre ranch on the Moon itself, free and clear; the second prize is a six-foot scale model of the actual Moon-ship, and there are fifty – count them – fifty third prizes, each a saddle-trained Shetland pony. Your hundred-word composition "Why I want to go to the Moon" will be judged for sincerity and originality, not on literary merit. Send those box-tops to Uncle Taffy, Box 214, Juarez, Old Mexico.'

Harriman was shown into the office of the president of the Moka-Cola Company ('Only a Moke is truly a coke' – 'Drink the Cola drink with the Lift'). He paused at the door, some twenty feet from the president's desk, and quickly pinned a two-inch-wide button to his lapel.

Patterson Griggs looked up. 'Well, this is really an honour, D. D. Do come in and —' The soft-drink executive stopped suddenly, his expression changed. 'What are you doing wearing *that*?' he snapped. 'Trying to annoy me?'

'That' was the two-inch disc; Harriman unpinned it and put it in his pocket. It was a circular advertising badge, in plain yellow; printed on it in black, almost covering it, was the symbol 6+, the trademark of Moka-Cola's only serious rival.

'No,' answered Harriman, 'though I don't blame you for being irritated. I see half the school kids in the country wearing these silly buttons. But I came to give you a friendly tip, not to annoy you.'

'What do you mean?'

'When I paused at your door, that badge on my lapel was just the size – to you, standing at your desk – the full Moon looks when you are standing in your garden, looking up at it. You didn't have any trouble reading what was on the badge, did you? I know you didn't; you yelled at me before either one of us stirred.'

'What about it?'

'How would you feel – and what would the effect be on your sales – if there was 'six-plus' written across the face of the Moon instead of just on a school-kid's sweater?'

Griggs thought about it, then said, 'D. D., don't make poor jokes; I've had a bad day.'

'I'm not joking. As you have probably heard around the Street, I'm behind this Moon-trip venture. Between ourselves, Pat, it's quite an expensive undertaking, even for me. A few days ago a man came to me – you'll pardon me if I don't mention names? You can figure it out. Anyhow, this man represented a client who wanted to buy the advertising concession for the Moon. He knew we weren't sure of success; but he said his client would take the risk.

'At first I couldn't figure out what he was talking about; he set me straight. Then I thought he was kidding. Then I was shocked. Look at this—' Harriman took out a large sheet of paper and spread it on Griggs's desk. 'You see the equipment is set up anywhere near the centre of the Moon, as we see it. Eighteen pyrotechnics rockets shoot out in eighteen directions, like the spokes of a wheel, but to carefully calculated distances. They hit and the bombs they carry go off, spreading finely divided carbon black for calculated distances. There's no air on the Moon, you know, Pat – a fine powder will throw just as easily as a javelin. Here's your result.' He turned the paper over; on the back there was a picture of the Moon, printed lightly. Overlaying it, in black, heavy print was 6+.

'So it *is* that outfit – those poisoners!'

'No, no, I didn't say so! But it illustrates the point; six-plus is only two symbols; it can be spread large enough to be read on the face of the Moon.'

Griggs stared at the horrid advertisement. 'I don't believe it will work!'

'A reliable pyrotechnics firm has guaranteed that it will – provided I can deliver their equipment to the spot. After all, Pat, it doesn't take much of a pyrotechnics rocket to go a long distance on the Moon. Why, you could throw a baseball a couple of miles yourself – low gravity, you know.'

'People would never stand for it. It's sacrilege!'

Harriman looked sad. 'I wish you were right. But they stand for skywriting – and video commercials.'

Griggs chewed his lips. 'Well, I don't see why you come to me with it,' he exploded. 'You know damn well the name of my product won't go on the face of the Moon. The letters would be too small to be read.'

Harriman nodded. 'That's exactly why I came to you. Pat, this isn't just a business venture to me; it's my heart and soul. It just made me sick to think of somebody actually wanting to use the face of the Moon for advertising. As you say, it's sacrilege. But somehow these jackals found out I was pressed for cash. They came to me when they knew I would have to listen.

'I put them off. I promised them an answer on Thursday. Then I went home and lay awake about it. After a while I thought of you.'

'Me?'

'You. You and your company. After all, you've got a good product and you need legitimate advertising for it. It occurred to me that there are more ways to use the Moon in advertising than by defacing it. Now just suppose that your company bought the same concession, but with the public-spirited promise of never letting it be used. Suppose you featured that fact in your ads? Suppose you ran pictures of a boy and girl, sitting out under the Moon, sharing a bottle of Moke? Suppose Moke was the only soft drink carried on the first trip to the Moon? But I don't have to tell you how to do it.' He glanced at his watch-finger. 'I've got to run and I don't want to rush you. If you want to do business, just leave word at my office by noon tomorrow and I'll have our man Montgomery get in touch with your advertising chief.'

The head of the big newspaper chain kept him waiting the minimum time reserved for tycoons and Cabinet members. Again Harriman stopped at the threshold of a large office and fixed a disc to his lapel.

'Howdy, Delos,' the publisher said. 'How's the traffic in green cheese today?' He then caught sight of the button and frowned. 'If that is a joke, it is in poor taste.'

Harriman pocketed the disc; it displayed not 6+, but the hammer-and-sickle.

'No,' he said, 'it's not a joke; it's a nightmare. Colonel, you and I are among the few people in this country who realize that communism is still a menace.'

Sometime later they were talking as chummily as if the Colonel's chain had not obstructed the Moon venture since its inception. The publisher waved a cigar at his desk. 'How did you come by those plans? Steal them?'

'They were copied,' Harriman answered with narrow truth. 'But they aren't important. The important thing is to get there first; we can't risk having an enemy rocket base on the moon. For years I've had a recurrent nightmare of waking up and seeing headlines that the Russians had landed on the Moon and declared the Lunar Soviet – say thirteen men and two female scientists – and had petitioned for entrance into the USSR – and that the petition had, of course, been graciously granted by the Supreme Soviet. I used to wake up and tremble. I don't know that they would actually go through with painting a hammer-and-sickle on the face of the Moon, but it's consistent with their psychology. Look at those enormous posters they are always hanging up.'

The publisher bit down hard on his cigar. 'We'll see what we can work out. Is there any way you can speed up your take-off?'

6

'Mr Harriman?'

'Yes?'

'That Mr LeCroix is here again.'

'Tell him I can't see him.'

'Yes, sir – uh, Mr Harriman, he did not mention it the other day but he says he is a rocket pilot.'

'Damn it, send him round to Skyways. I don't hire pilots.'

A man's face crowded into the screen, displacing Harriman's reception secretary. 'Mr Harriman – I'm Leslie Le-Croix, relief pilot of the *Charon*.'

'I don't care if you are the Angel Gab. Did you say *Charon*?'

'I said *Charon*. And I've got to talk to you.'

'Come in.'

Harriman greeted his visitor, offered him tobacco, then looked him over with interest. The *Charon*, shuttle rocket to the lost power satellite, had been the nearest thing to a spaceship the world had yet seen. Its pilot, lost in the same explosion that had destroyed the satellite and the *Charon*, had been the first, in a way, of the coming breed of spacemen.

Harriman wondered how it had escaped his attention that the *Charon* had alternating pilots. He had known it, of course – but somehow he had forgotten to take the fact into account. He had written off the power satellite, its shuttle rocket and everything about it, ceased to think about them. He now looked at LeCroix with curiosity.

He saw a small, neat man with a thin, intelligent face, and the big, competent hands of a jockey. LeCroix returned his inspection without embarrassment. He seemed calm and utterly sure of himself.

'Well, Captain LeCroix?'

'You are building a Moon-ship.'

'Who says so?'

'A Moon-ship is being built. The boys all say you are behind it.'

'Yes?'

'I want to pilot it.'

'Why should you?'

'I'm the best man for it.'

Harriman paused to let out a cloud of tobacco smoke. 'If you can prove that, the billet is yours.'

'It's a deal.' LeCroix stood up. 'I'll leave my name and address outside.'

'Wait a minute. I said "if". Let's talk. I'm going along on this trip myself; I want to know more about you before I trust my neck to you.'

They discussed Moon flight, interplanetary travel, rocketry, what they might find on the Moon. Gradually Harriman warmed up, as he found another spirit so like his own, so obsessed with the Wonderful Dream. Subconsciously he had already accepted LeCroix; the conversation began to assume that it would be a joint venture.

After a long time Harriman said, 'This is fun, Les, but I've got to do a few chores yet today, or none of us will get to the Moon. You go on out to Peterson Field and get acquainted with Bob Coster – I'll call him. If the pair of you can manage to get along, we'll talk contract.' He scribbled a chit and handed it to LeCroix. 'Give this to Miss Perkins as you go out and she'll put you on the pay-roll.'

'That can wait.'

'Man's got to eat.'

LeCroix accepted it, but did not leave. 'There's one thing I don't understand, Mr Harriman.'

'Huh?'

'Why are you planning on a chemically powered ship?

Not that I object; I'll herd her. But why do it the hard way? I know you had the *City of Brisbane* refitted for X-fuel —'

Harriman stared at him. 'Are you off your nut, Les? You're asking why pigs don't have wings – there isn't any X-fuel, and there won't be any more until we make some ourselves – on the Moon.'

'Who told you that?'

'What do you mean?'

'The way I heard it, the Atomic Energy Commission allocated X-fuel, under treaty, to several other countries – and some of them weren't prepared to make use of it. But they got it just the same. What happened to it?'

'Oh, *that*! Sure, Les, several of the little outfits in Central America and South America were cut in for a slice of pie for political reasons, even though they had no way to eat it. A good thing, too – we bought it back and used it to ease the immediate power shortage.' Harriman frowned. 'You're right, though. I should have grabbed some of the stuff then.'

'And you *sure* it's all gone?'

'Why, of course, I'm— No, I'm not. I'll look into it. G'bye, Les.'

His contacts were able to account for every pound of X-fuel in short order – save for Costa Rica's allotment. That nation had declined to sell back its supply because its power plant, suitable for X-fuel, had been almost finished at the time of the disaster. Another inquiry disclosed that the power plant had never been finished.

Montgomery was even then in Managua; Nicaragua had had a change in administration and Montgomery was making certain that the special position of the local Moon corporation was protected. Harriman sent him a coded message to proceed to San José, locate X-fuel, buy it and ship it back – at any cost. He then went to see the chairman of the Atomic Energy Commission.

That official was apparently glad to see him and anxious to be affable. Harriman got around to explaining that he wanted a licence to do experimental work in isotopes – X-fuel, to be precise.

'This should be brought up through the usual channels,

Mr Harriman.'

'It will be. This is a preliminary inquiry. I want to know your reactions.'

'After all, I am not the only commissioner ... and we almost always follow the recommendations of our technical branch.'

'Don't fence with me, Carl. You know durn well you control a working majority. Off the record, what do you say?'

'Well, D. D. – off the record – you can't get any X-fuel, so why get a licence?'

'Let me worry about that.'

'Mmmm ... we weren't required by law to follow every millicurie of X-fuel, since it isn't classed as potentially suitable for mass weapons. Just the same, we knew what happened to it. There's none available.'

Harriman kept quiet.

'In the second place, you can have an X-fuel licence, if you wish – for any purpose but rocket fuel.'

'Why the restriction?'

'You are building a Moon-ship, aren't you?'

'Me?'

'Don't *you* fence with me, D. D. It's my business to know things. You can't use X-fuel for rockets, even if you can find it – which you can't.' The chairman went to a vault back of his desk and returned with a quarto volume, which he laid in front of Harriman. It was titled: *Theoretical Investigations into the Stability of Several Radioisotopic Fuels – with Notes on the* Charon-*Power-Satellite Disaster*. The cover had a serial number and was stamped: *SECRET*.

Harriman pushed it away. 'I've got no business looking at that – and I wouldn't understand it if I did.'

The chairman grinned. 'Very well, I'll tell you what's in it. I'm deliberately tying your hands, D. D., by trusting you with a defence secret—'

'I won't have it, I tell you!'

'Don't try to power a space-ship with X-fuel, D. D. It's a lovely fuel – but it may go off like a firecracker anywhere out in space. That report tells why.'

'Confound it, we ran the *Charon* for nearly three years!'

'You were lucky. It is the official – but utterly confidential – opinion of the Government that the *Charon* set off

94

the power satellite, rather than the satellite setting off the *Charon*. We had thought it was the other way around at first, and of course it could have been, but there was the disturbing matter of the radar records. It seemed as if the ship had gone up a split second before the satellite. So we made an intensive theoretical investigation. X-fuel is too dangerous for rockets.'

'That's ridiculous! For every pound burned in the *Charon* there were at least a hundred pounds used in power plants on the surface. How come *they* didn't explode?'

'It's a matter of shielding. A rocket necessarily uses less shielding than a stationary plant, but the worst feature is that it operates out in space. The disaster is presumed to have been triggered by primary cosmic radiation. If you like, I'll call in one of the mathematical physicists to elucidate.'

Harriman shook his head. 'You know I don't speak the language.' He considered. 'I suppose that's all there is to it?'

'I'm afraid so. I'm really sorry.' Harriman got up to leave. 'Uh, one more thing, D. D. – you weren't thinking of approaching any of my subordinate colleagues, were you?'

'Of course not. Why should I?'

'I'm glad to hear it. You know, Mr Harriman, some of our staff may not be the most brilliant scientists in the world – it's very hard to keep a first-class scientist happy in the conditions of government service. But there is one thing I am sure of: all of them are utterly incorruptible. Knowing that, I would take it as a personal affront if anyone tried to influence one of my people – a very personal affront.'

'So?'

'Yes. By the way, I used to box light-heavyweight in college. I've kept it up.'

'Hmmm ... well, I never went to college. But I play a fair game of poker.' Harriman suddenly grinned. 'I won't tamper with your boys, Carl. It would be too much like offering a bribe to a starving man. Well, so long.'

When Harriman got back to his office he called in one of his confidential clerks. 'Take another coded message to Mr Montgomery. Tell him to ship the stuff to Panama City, rather than to the States.' He started to dictate another message to Coster, intending to tell him to stop work on the *Pioneer*, whose skeleton was already reaching skyward on the Colorado prairie, and shift to the *Santa Maria*, formerly the *City of Brisbane*.

He thought better of it. Take-off would have to be outside the United States; with the Atomic Energy Commission acting stuffy, it would not do to try to move the *Santa Maria*: it would give the show away.

Nor could she be moved without refitting her for chempowered flight. No, he would have another ship of the *Brisbane* class taken out of service and sent to Panama, and the power plant of the *Santa Maria* could be disassembled and shipped there, too. Coster could have the new ship ready in six weeks, maybe sooner ... and he, Coster, and LeCroix would start for the Moon!

The devil with worries over primary cosmic rays! The *Charon* operated for three years, didn't she? They would take the trip, they would prove it could be done, then, if safer fuels were needed, there would be the incentive to dig them out. The important thing was to do it, make the trip. If Columbus had waited for decent ships, we'd all still be in Europe. A man had to take some chances, or he never got anywhere.

Contentedly he started drafting the messages that would get the new scheme under way.

He was interrupted by a secretary. 'Mr Harriman, Mr Montgomery wants to speak to you.'

'Eh? Has he got my code already?'

'I don't know, sir.'

'Well, put him on.'

Montgomery had not received the second message. But he had news for Harriman: Costa Rica had sold all its X-fuel to the English Ministry of Power, soon after the disaster. There was not an ounce of it left, neither in Costa Rica, nor in England.

Harriman sat and moped for several minutes after Montgomery had cleared the screen. Then he called Coster. 'Bob, is LeCroix there?'

'Right here – we were about to go out to dinner together. Here he is, now.'

'Howdy, Les. Les, that was a good brain-storm of yours,

but it didn't work. Somebody stole the baby.'

'Eh? Oh, I get you. I'm sorry.'

'Don't ever waste time being sorry. We'll go ahead as originally planned. We'll get there!'

'Sure we will.'

7

From the June issue of *Popular Technics* magazine: 'URANIUM PROSPECTING ON THE MOON – a Fact Article about a soon-to-come Major Industry.'

From HOLIDAY: *'Honeymoon on the Moon* – A Discussion of the Miracle Resort that your children will enjoy, as told to our travel editor.'

From the *American Sunday Magazine* – 'DIAMONDS ON THE MOON?' – A World-famous Scientist Shows Why Diamonds Must be common as Pebbles in the Lunar Craters.'

'Of course, Clem, I don't know anything about electronics, but here is the way it was explained to me. You can hold the beam of a television broadcast down to a degree or so these days, can't you?'

'Yes – if you use a big enough reflector.'

'You'll have plenty of elbow room. Now, Earth covers a space two degrees wide, as seen from the Moon. Sure, it's quite a distance away, but you'd have no power losses and absolutely perfect and unchanging conditions for transmission. Once you made your set-up, it wouldn't be any more expensive than broadcasting from the top of a mountain here, and a durned sight less expensive than keeping copters in the air from coast to coast, the way you're having to do now.'

'It's a fantastic scheme, Delos.'

'What's fantastic about it? Getting to the Moon is my worry, not yours. Once we are there, there's going to be television back to Earth; you can bet your shirt on that. It's a natural set-up for line-of-sight transmission. If you aren't interested, I'll have to find someone who is.'

'I didn't say I wasn't interested.'

'Well, make up your mind. Here's another thing, Clem – I don't want to go sticking my nose into your business, but haven't you had a certain amount of trouble since you lost the use of the power satellite as a relay station?'

'You know the answer; don't needle me. Expenses have gone out of sight without any improvement in revenue.'

'That wasn't quite what I meant. How about censorship?'

The television executive threw up his hands. 'Don't use that word! How anybody expects a man to stay in business with every two-bit wowser in the country claiming a veto over what we can say and can't say and what we can show and what we can't show – it's enough to make you throw up. The whole principle is wrong; it's like demanding that grown men live on skim milk because the baby can't eat steak. If I were able to lay my hands on those confounded, prurient-minded slimy—'

'Easy! easy!' Harriman interrupted. 'Did it ever occur to you that there is absolutely no way to interfere with a telecast from the Moon – and that boards of censorship on Earth won't have jurisdiction in any case?'

'What? Say that again.'

' "LIFE goes to the Moon." LIFE-TIME Inc. is proud to announce that arrangements have been completed to bring LIFE's readers a personally conducted tour of the first trip to our satellite. In place of the usual weekly feature "LIFE goes to a Party" there will commence, immediately after the return of the first successful—'

'ASSURANCE FOR THE NEW AGE.'

(An excerpt from an advertisement of the North Atlantic Mutual Insurance and Liability Company.)

'– the same looking-to-the-future that protected our policy-holders after the Chicago Fire, after the San Francisco Fire, after every disaster since the War of 1812, now reaches out to insure you from unexpected loss *even on the Moon*—'

'THE UNBOUNDED FRONTIERS OF TECHNOLOGY.'

'When the Moon-ship *Pioneer* climbs skyward on a ladder of flame, twenty-seven essential devices in her "innards" will be powered by especially engineered DELTA batteries —'

'Mr Harriman, could you come out to the field?'

'What's up, Bob?'

'Trouble,' Coster answered briefly.

'What sort of trouble?'

Coster hesitated. 'I'd rather not talk about it by screen. If you can't come, maybe Les and I had better come there.'

'I'll be there this evening.'

When Harriman got there he saw that LeCroix's impassive face concealed bitterness, Coster looked stubborn and defensive. He waited until the three were alone in Coster's workroom before he spoke. 'Let's have it, boys.'

LeCroix looked at Coster. The engineer chewed his lip and said, 'Mr Harriman, you know the stages this design has been through.'

'More or less.'

'We had to give up the catapult idea. Then we had this —' Coster rummaged on his desk, pulled out a perspective treatment of a four-step rocket, large but rather graceful. 'Theoretically it was a possibility; practically it cut things too fine. By the time the stress group boys and the auxiliary group and the control group got through adding things, we were forced to come to this —' He hauled out another sketch; it was basically like the first, but squatter, almost pyramidal. 'We added a fifth stage as a ring around the fourth stage. We even managed to save some weight by using most of the auxiliary and control equipment for the fourth stage to control the fifth stage. And it still had enough sectional density to punch through the atmosphere with no important drag, even if it was clumsy.'

Harriman nodded. 'You know, Bob, we're going to have to get away from the step-rocket idea before we set up a scheduled run to the Moon.'

'I don't see how you can avoid it with chem-powered rockets.'

'If you had a decent catapult you could put a single-stage chem-powered rocket into an orbit around the Earth, couldn't you?'

'Sure.'

'That's what we'll do. Then it will refuel in that orbit.'

'The old space-station set-up. I suppose that makes sense – in fact I know it does. Only the ship wouldn't refuel and continue on to the Moon. The economical thing would be to have special ships that never landed anywhere make the jump from there to another fuelling station around the Moon. Then —'

LeCroix displayed a most unusual impatience. 'All that doesn't mean anything now. Get on with the story, Bob.'

'Right,' agreed Harriman.

'Well, this model should have done it. And, damn it, it still should do it.'

Harriman looked puzzled. 'But, Bob, that's the approved design, isn't it? That's what you've got two-thirds built right out there on the field.'

'Yes,' Coster looked stricken. 'But it won't do it. It won't work.'

'Why not?'

'Because I've had to add in too much dead weight, that's why. Mr Harriman, you aren't an engineer; you've no idea how fast the performance falls off when you have to clutter up a ship with anything but fuel and power plant. Take the landing arrangements for the fifth-stage power ring. You use that stage for a minute and a half, then you throw it away. But you don't dare take a chance of it falling on Wichita or Kansas City. We have to include a parachute sequence. Even then we have to plan on tracking it by radar and cutting the shrouds by radio control when it's over empty countryside and not too high. That means more weight, besides the parachute. By the time we are through we don't get a net addition of a mile a second out of that stage. It's not enough.'

Harriman stirred in his chair. 'Looks like we made a mistake in trying to launch it from the States. Suppose we took off from someplace unpopulated – say the Brazil coast – and let the booster stages fall in the Atlantic; how much would that save you?'

Coster looked off in the distance, then took out a slide rule. 'Might work.'

'How much of a chore will it be to move the ship at this stage?'

'Well ... it would have to be disassembled completely; nothing less would do. I can't give you a cost estimate off-hand, but it would be expensive.'

'How long would it take?'

'Hmm ... shucks, Mr Harriman, I can't answer off-hand. Two years – eighteen months, with luck. We'd have to prepare a site. We'd have to build shops.'

Harriman thought about it, although he knew the answer in his heart. His shoe-string, big as it was, was stretched to the danger point. He couldn't keep up the promotion, on talk alone, for another two years; he *had* to have a successful flight and soon – or the whole jerry-built financial structure would burst. 'No good, Bob.'

'I was afraid of that. Well, I tried to add still a sixth stage.' He held up another sketch. 'You see that monstrosity? I reached the point of diminishing returns. The final effective velocity is actually less with this abortion than with the five-step job.'

'Does that mean you are whipped, Bob? You can't build a Moon-ship?'

'No, I —'

LeCroix said suddenly, 'Clear out Kansas.'

'Eh?' asked Harriman.

'Clear everybody out of Kansas and Eastern Colorado. Let the fifth and fourth sections fall anywhere in that area. The third section falls in the Atlantic; the second section goes into permanent orbit – and the ship itself goes on to the Moon. You could do it if you didn't have to waste weight on the parachuting of the fifth and fourth sections. Ask Bob.'

'So? How about it, Bob?'

'That's what I said before. It was the parasitic penalties that whipped us. The basic design is all right.'

'Hmmm ... somebody hand me an atlas.' Harriman looked up Kansas and Colorado, did some rough figuring. He stared off into space, looking surprisingly, for the moment, as Coster did when the engineer was thinking about his own work. Finally he said, 'It won't work.'

'Why not?'

'Money. I told you not to worry about money – for the ship. But it would cost upwards of six or seven million

101

dollars to evacuate that area even for a day. We'd have to settle nuisance suits out of hand; we couldn't wait. And there would be a few diehards who just wouldn't move anyhow.'

LeCroix said savagely, 'If the crazy fools won't move, let them take their chances.'

'I know how you feel, Les. But this project is too big to hide and too big to move. Unless we protect the bystanders we'll be shut down by court order and force. I can't buy all the judges in two states. Some of them wouldn't be for sale.'

'It was a nice try, Les,' consoled Coster.

'I thought it might be an answer for all of us,' the pilot answered.

Harriman said, 'You were starting to mention another solution, Bob?'

Coster looked embarrassed. 'You know the plans for the ship itself – a three-man job, space and supplies for three.'

'Yes. What are you driving at?'

'It doesn't have to be three men. Split the first step into two parts, cut the ship down to the bare minimum for one man and jettison the remainder. That's the only way I see to make this basic design work.' He got out another sketch. 'See? One man and supplies for less than a week. No airlock – the pilot stays in his pressure suit. No galley. No bunks. The bare minimum to keep one man alive for a maximum of two hundred hours. It will work.'

'It will work,' repeated LeCroix, looking at Coster.

Harriman looked at the sketch with an odd, sick feeling in his stomach. Yes, no doubt it would work – and for the purposes of the promotion it did not matter whether one man or three went to the Moon and returned. Just to do it was enough; he was dead certain that one successful flight would cause money to roll in, so that there would be capital to develop to the point of practical passenger-carrying ships.

The Wright brothers had started with less.

'If that is what I have to put up with, I suppose I have to,' he said slowly.

Coster looked relieved. 'Fine! But there is one more hitch. You know the conditions under which I agreed to tackle this job – I was to go along. Now Les here waves a contract under my nose and says *he* has to be the pilot.'

'It's not just that,' LeCroix countered. 'You're no pilot, Bob. You'll kill yourself and ruin the whole enterprise, just through bull-headed stubbornness.'

'I'll learn to fly it. After all, I designed it. Look here, Mr Harriman. I hate to let you in for a suit – Les says he will sue – but my contract antedates his. I intend to enforce it.'

'Don't listen to him, Mr Harriman. Let him do the suing. I'll fly the ship and bring her back. He'll wreck it.'

'Either I go or I don't build the ship,' Coster said flatly.

Harriman motioned both of them to keep quiet. 'Easy, easy, both of you. You can both sue me if it gives you any pleasure. Bob, don't talk nonsense; at this stage I can hire other engineers to finish the job. You tell me it has to be just one man.'

'That's right.'

'You're looking at him.'

They both stared.

'Shut your jaws,' Harriman snapped. 'What's funny about that? You both knew I meant to go. You don't think I went to all this trouble just to give you two a ride to the Moon, do you? *I intend to go.* What's wrong with me as a pilot? I'm in good health, my eyesight is all right, I'm still smart enough to learn what I have to learn. If I have to drive my own buggy, I'll do it. I won't step aside for anybody, not anybody, d'you hear me?'

Coster got his breath first. 'Boss, you don't know what you are saying.'

Two hours later they were still wrangling. Most of the time Harriman had stubbornly sat still, refusing to answer their arguments. At last he went out of the room for a few minutes, on the usual pretext. When he came back in he said, 'Bob, what do you weigh?'

'Me? A little over two hundred.'

'Close to two twenty, I'd judge. Les, what do you weigh?'

'One twenty-six.'

'Bob, design the ship for a net load of one hundred and twenty-six pounds.'

'Huh? Now wait a minute. Mr Harriman —'

'*Shut up!* If I can't learn to be a pilot in six weeks, neither can you.'

'But I've got the mathematics and the basic knowledge to —'

'Shut up, I said! Les has spent as long learning his profession as you have learning yours. Can he become an engineer in six weeks? Then what gave you the conceit to think that you can learn his job in that time? I'm not going to have you wrecking my ship to satisfy your swollen ego. Anyhow, you gave out the real key to it when you were discussing the design. The real limiting factor is the actual weight of the passenger or passengers, isn't it? Everything – *everything* works in proportion to that one mass. Right?'

'Yes, but —'

'Right or wrong?'

'Well ... yes, that's right. I just wanted —'

'The smaller man can live on less water, he breathes less air, he occupies less space. Les goes.' Harriman walked over and put a hand on Coster's shoulder. 'Don't take it hard, son. It can't be any worse on you than it is on me. This trip has got to succeed – and that means you and I have got to give up the honour of being the first man on the Moon. But I promise you this: we'll go on the second trip, we'll go with Les as our private chauffeur. It will be the first of a lot of passenger trips. Look, Bob – you can be a big man in this game, if you'll play along now. How would you like to be Chief Engineer of the first lunar colony?'

Coster managed to grin. 'It might not be so bad.'

'You'd like it. Living on the Moon will be an engineering problem; you and I have talked about it. How'd you like to put your theories to work? Build the first city? Build the big observatory we'll found there? Look around and know that you were the man who had done it?'

Coster was definitely adjusting himself to it. 'You make it sound good. Say, what will *you* be doing?'

'Me? Well, maybe I'll be the first mayor of Luna City.' It was a new thought to him; he savoured it. 'The Honourable Delos David Harriman, Mayor of Luna City. Say, I like that! You know, I've never held any sort of public office; I've just owned things.' He looked around. 'Everything settled?'

'I guess so,' Coster said slowly. Suddenly he stuck his hand out at LeCroix. 'You fly her, Les; I'll build her.'

LeCroix grabbed his hand. 'It's a deal. And you and the Boss get busy and start making plans for the next job – big enough for all of us.'

'Right!'

Harriman put his hand on top of theirs. 'That's the way I like to hear you talk. We'll stick together and we'll found Luna City together.'

'I think we ought to call it "Harriman",' LeCroix said seriously.

'Nope, I've thought of it as Luna City ever since I was a kid; Luna City it's going to be. Maybe we'll put Harriman Square in the middle of it,' he added.

'I'll mark it that way in the plans,' agreed Coster.

Harriman left at once. Despite the solution he was terribly depressed and did not want his colleagues to see it. It had been a Pyrrhic victory; he had saved the enterprise, but he felt like an animal who has gnawed off his own leg to escape a trap.

8

Strong was alone in the offices of the partnership when he got a call from Dixon. 'George, I was looking for D. D. Is he there?'

'No, he's back in Washington – something about clearances. I expect him back soon.'

'Hmmm ... Entenza and I want to see him. We're coming over.'

They arrived shortly. Entenza was quite evidently very much worked up over something; Dixon looked sleekly impassive, as usual. After greetings Dixon waited a moment, then said, 'Jack, you had some business to transact, didn't you?'

Entenza jumped, then snatched a draft from his pocket. 'Oh, yes! George, I'm not going to have a pro-rate, after all. Here's my payment to bring my share up to full payment to date.'

Strong accepted it. 'I know that Delos will be pleased.'

' He tucked it in a drawer.

'Well,' said Dixon sharply, 'aren't you going to receipt for it?'

'If Jack wants a receipt. The cancelled draft will serve.' However, Strong wrote out a receipt without further comment; Entenza accepted it.

They waited a while. Presently Dixon said, 'George, you're in this pretty deep, aren't you?'

'Possibly.'

'Want to hedge your bets?'

'How?'

'Well, candidly, I want to protect myself. Want to sell one half of one per cent of your share?'

Strong thought about it. In fact he was worried – worried sick. The presence of Dixon's auditor had forced them to keep on a cash basis – and only Strong knew how close to the line that had forced the partners. 'Why do you want it?'

'Oh, I wouldn't use it to interfere with Delos's operations. He's our man; we're backing him. But I would feel a lot safer if I had the right to call a halt if he tried to commit us to something we couldn't pay for. You know Delos; he's an incurable optimist. We ought to have some sort of a brake on him.'

Strong thought about it. The thing that hurt him was that he agreed with everything Dixon said; he had stood by and watched while Delos dissipated two fortunes, painfully built up through the years. D. D. no longer seemed to care. Why, only this morning he had refused even to look at a report on the H & S automatic household switch – after dumping it on Strong.

Dixon leaned forward. 'Name a price, George. I'll be generous.'

Strong squared his shoulders. 'I'll sell —'

'Good!'

'– if Delos okays it. Not otherwise.'

Dixon muttered something. Entenza snorted. The conversation might have gone acrimoniously further, had not Harriman walked in.

No one said anything about the proposal to Strong. Strong inquired about the trip; Harriman pressed a thumb

106

and finger together. 'All in the groove! But it gets more expensive to do business in Washington every day.' He turned to the others. 'How's tricks? Any special meaning to the assemblage? Are we in executive session?'

Dixon turned to Entenza. 'Tell him, Jack.'

Entenza faced Harriman. 'What do you mean by selling television rights?'

Harriman cocked a brow. 'And why not?'

'Because you promised them to me, that's why. That's the original agreement; I've got it in writing.'

'Better take another look at the agreement, Jack. And don't go off half-cocked. You have the exploitation rights for radio, television, and other amusement and special feature ventures in connexion with the first trip to the Moon. You've still got 'em. Including broadcasts from the ship, provided we are able to make any.' He decided that this was not a good time to mention that weight consideration had already made the latter impossible; the *Pioneer* would carry no electronic equipment of any sort not needed in astrogation. 'What I sold was the franchise to erect a television station on the Moon, later. By the way, it wasn't even an exclusive franchise, although Clem Haggerty thinks it is. If you want to buy one yourself, we can accommodate you.'

'*Buy* it! Why, you —'

'Wups! Or you can have it free, if you can get Dixon and George to agree that you are entitled to it. I won't be a tight wad. Anything else?'

Dixon cut in. 'Just where do we stand now, Delos?'

'Gentlemen, you can take it for granted that the *Pioneer* will leave on schedule – next Wednesday. And now, if you will excuse me, I'm on my way to Peterson Field.'

After he had left, his three associates sat in silence for some time, Entenza muttering to himself, Dixon apparently thinking, and Strong just waiting. Presently Dixon said, 'How about that fractional share, George?'

'You didn't see fit to mention it to Delos.'

'I see.' Dixon carefully deposited an ash. 'He's a strange man, isn't he?'

Strong shifted around. 'Yes.'

'How long have you known him?'

'Let me see – he came to work for me in —'

'*He* worked for *you*?'

'For several months. Then we set up our first company.' Strong thought back about it. 'I suppose he had a power complex, even then.'

'No,' Dixon said carefully. 'No, I wouldn't call it a power complex. It's more of a Messiah complex.'

Entenza looked up. 'He's a crooked son of a bitch, that's what he is!'

Strong looked at him mildly. 'I'd rather you wouldn't talk about him that way. I'd really rather you wouldn't.'

'Stow it, Jack,' ordered Dixon. 'You might force George to take a poke at you. One of the odd things about him,' went on Dixon, 'is that he seems to be able to inspire an almost feudal loyalty. Take yourself. I know you are cleaned out, George – yet you won't let me rescue you. That goes beyond logic; it's personal.'

Strong nodded. 'He's an odd man. Sometimes I think he's the last of the Robber Barons.'

Dixon shook his head. 'Not the last. The last of them opened up the American West. He's the first of the *new* Robber Barons – and you and I won't see the end of it. Do you ever read Carlyle?'

Strong nodded again. 'I see what you mean, the "Hero" theory; but I don't necessarily agree with it.'

'There's something to it, though,' Dixon answered. 'Truthfully, I don't think Delos knows what he is doing. He's setting up a new imperialism. There'll be hell to pay before it's cleaned up.' He stood up. 'Maybe we should have waited. Maybe we should have baulked him – *if* we could have. Well, it's done. We're on the merry-go-round and we can't get off. I hope we enjoy the ride. Come on, Jack.'

9

The Colorado prairie was growing dusky. The Sun was behind the peak, and the broad white face of Luna, full and round, was rising in the east. In the middle of Peterson Field the *Pioneer* thrust towards the sky. A barbed-wire fence, a thousand yards from its base in all directions, held back the crowds. Just inside the barrier guards patrolled restlessly. More guards circulated through the crowd. Inside the fence, close to it, trucks and trailers for camera, sound, and television equipment were parked, and at the far ends of cables remote-control pick-ups were located near and far from the ship on all sides. There were other trucks near the ship and a stir of organized activity.

Harriman waited in Coster's office; Coster himself was out on the field, and Dixon and Entenza had a room to themselves. LeCroix, still in a drugged sleep, was in the bedroom of Coster's on-the-job living quarters.

There was a stir and a challenge outside the door. Harriman opened it a crack. 'If that's another reporter, tell him "no". Send him to Mr Montgomery across the way. Captain LeCroix will grant no unauthorized interviews.'

'Delos! Let me in.'

'Oh – you, George. Come in. We've been hounded to death.'

Strong came in and handed Harriman a large and heavy handbag. 'Here it is.'

'Here is what?'

'The cancelled covers for the philatelic syndicate. You forgot them. That's half a million dollars, Delos,' he complained. 'If I hadn't noticed them in your coat locker we'd have been in the soup.'

Harriman composed his features. 'George, you're a brick; that's what you are.'

'Shall I put them in the ship myself?' Strong asked anxiously.

'Huh? No, no. Les will handle them.' He glanced at his watch. 'We're about to waken him. I'll take charge of the covers.' He took the bag and added, 'Don't come in now. You'll have a chance to say good-bye on the field.'

Harriman went next door, shut the door behind him, waited for the nurse to give the sleeping pilot a counteracting stimulant by injection, then chased her out. When he turned around the pilot was sitting up, rubbing his eyes. 'How do you feel, Les?'

'Fine. So this is it.'

'Yup. And we're all rooting for you, boy. Look, you've got to go out and face them in a couple of minutes. Everything is ready – but I've got a couple of things I've got to say to you.'

'Yes?'

'See this bag?' Harriman rapidly explained what it was and what it signified.

LeCroix looked dismayed. 'But I *can't* take it, Delos. It's all figured to the last ounce.'

'Who said you were going to take it? Of course you can't; it must weigh sixty, seventy pounds. I just plain forgot it. Now here's what we do: for the time being I'll hide it in here —' Harriman stuffed the bag far back into a clothes closet. 'When you land, I'll be right on your tail. Then we pull a sleight-of-hand trick and you fetch it out of the ship.'

LeCroix shook his head ruefully. 'Delos, you beat me. Well, I'm in no mood to argue.'

'I'm glad you're not; otherwise I'd go to jail for a measly half-million dollars. We've already spent that money. Anyhow, it doesn't matter,' he went on. 'Nobody but you and me will know it – and the stamp collectors will get their money's worth.' He looked at the younger man as if anxious for his approval.

'Okay, okay,' LeCroix answered. 'Why should I care what happens to a stamp collector – tonight? Let's get going.'

'One more thing,' said Harriman and took out a small cloth bag. 'This you take with you – and the weight *has* been figured in. I saw to it. Now here is what you do with it.' He gave detailed and very earnest instructions.

LeCroix was puzzled. 'Do I hear you straight? I let it be found – then I tell the exact truth about what happened?'

'That's right.'

'Okay.' LeCroix zipped the little bag into a pocket of his overalls. 'Let's get out to the field. H-hour minus twenty-one minutes already.'

Strong joined Harriman in the control blockhouse after LeCroix had gone up inside the ship. 'Did they get aboard?' he demanded anxiously. 'LeCroix wasn't carrying anything.'

'Oh, sure,' said Harriman. 'I sent them ahead. Better take your place. The ready flare has already gone up.'

Dixon, Entenza, the Governor of Colorado, the Vice-

110

President of the United States, and a round dozen of VIP's were already seated at periscopes, mounted in slits, on a balcony above the control level. Strong and Harriman climbed a ladder and took the two remaining chairs.

Harriman began to sweat, and realized he was trembling. Through his periscope out in front he could see the ship; from below he could hear Coster's voice, nervously checking departure station reports. Muted through a speaker by him was a running commentary of one of the newscasters reporting the show. Harriman himself was the – well, the admiral, he decided – of the operation, but there was nothing more he could do but wait, watch, and try to pray.

A second flare arched up in the sky, burst into red and green. Five minutes.

The seconds oozed away. At minus two minutes Harriman realized that he could not stand to watch through a tiny slit; he had to be outside, take part in it himself – he had to. He climbed down, hurried to the exit of the blockhouse. Coster glanced around, looked startled, but did not try to stop him. Coster could not leave his post, no matter what happened. Harriman elbowed the guard aside and went outdoors.

To the east the ship towered skyward, her slender pyramid sharp black against the full Moon. He waited.

And waited.

What had gone wrong? There had remained less than two minutes when he had come out; he was sure of that – yet there she stood, silent, dark, unmoving. There was not a sound, save the distant ululation of sirens warning the spectators behind the distant fence. Harriman felt his own heart stop, his breath dry up in his throat. Something had failed. Failure.

A single flare-rocket burst from the top of the blockhouse; a flame licked at the base of the ship.

It spread, there was a pad of white fire around the base. Slowly, almost lumberingly, the *Pioneer* lifted, seemed to hover for a moment, balanced on a pillar of fire – then reached for the sky with acceleration so great that she was above him almost at once, overhead at the zenith, a dazzling circle of flame. So quickly was she above, rather than out in front, that it seemed as if she were arching back over

111

him and must surely fall on him. Instinctively and futilely he threw a hand in front of his face.

The sound reached him.

Not as sound – it was a white noise, a roar in all frequencies, sonic, subsonic, supersonic, so incredibly loaded with energy that it struck him in the chest. He heard it with his teeth and with his bones, as well as with his ears. He crouched his knees, bracing against it.

Following the sound at the snail's pace of a hurricane came the backwash of the splash. It ripped at his clothing, tore his breath from his lips. He stumbled blindly back, trying to reach the lee of the concrete building, was knocked down.

He picked himself up coughing and strangling, and remembered to look at the sky. Straight overhead was a dwindling star. Then it was gone.

He went into the blockhouse.

The room was a babble of high-tension, purposeful confusion. Harriman's ears, still ringing, heard a speaker blare, 'Spot One! Spot One to blockhouse! Step five loose on schedule – ship and step five showing separate blips —' and Coster's voice, high and angry, cutting in with, 'Get Track One! Have they picked up step five yet? Are they tracking it?'

In the background the news commentator was still blowing his top. 'A great day, folks, a great day! The mighty *Pioneer*, climbing like an angel of the Lord, flaming sword at hand, is even now on her glorious way to our sister planet. Most of you have seen her departure on your screens; I wish you could have seen it as I did, arching up into the evening sky, bearing her precious load of —'

'Shut that damn thing off!' ordered Coster, then to the visitors on the observation platform, 'And pipe down up there! Quiet!'

The Vice-President of the United States jerked his head around, closed his mouth. He remembered to smile. The other VIPs shut up, then resumed again in muted whispers. A girl's voice cut through the silence, 'Track One to Blockhouse – step five tracking high, plus two.' There was a stir in the corner. There a large canvas hood shielded a heavy sheet of Plexiglass from direct light. The sheet was

112

mounted vertically and was edge-lighted; it displayed a co-ordinate map of Colorado and Kansas in fine white lines; the cities and towns glowed red. Unevacuated farms were tiny warning dots of red light.

A man behind the transparent map touched it with a grease pencil; the reported location of step five shone out. In front of the map screen a youngish man sat quietly in a chair, a pear-shaped switch in his hand, his thumb lightly resting on the button. He was a bombardier, borrowed from the Air Forces; when he pressed the switch, a radio-controlled circuit in step five should cause the shrouds of step five's landing 'chute to be cut and let it plummet to Earth. He was working from radar reports alone, with no fancy computing bombsight to think for him. He was working almost by instinct – or, rather, by the accumulated subconscious knowledge of his trade, integrating in his brain the meagre data spread before him, deciding where the tons of step five would land if he were to press his switch at any particular instant. He seemed unworried.

'Spot One to Blockhouse!' came a man's voice again. 'Step four free on schedule,' and almost immediately following, a deeper voice echoed, 'Track Two, tracking step four, instantaneous altitude nine-five-one miles, predicted vector.'

No one paid any attention to Harriman.

Under the hood the observed trajectory of step five grew in shining dots of grease, near to, but not on, the dotted line of its predicted path. Reaching out from each location dot was drawn a line at right angles, the reported altitude for that location.

The quiet man watching the display suddenly pressed down hard on his switch. He then stood up, stretched, and said, 'Anybody got a cigarette?' 'Track Two!' he was answered. 'Step four – first impact prediction – forty miles west of Charleston, South Carolina.'

'Repeat!' yelled Coster.

The speaker blared out again without pause, 'Correction, correction – forty miles east, repeat *east*.'

Coster sighed. The sigh was cut short by a report: 'Spot one to Blockhouse – step three free, minus five seconds,' and a talker at Coster's control desk called out, 'Mr Coster,

113

Mr Coster – Palomar Observatory wants to talk to you.'

'Tell 'em to go – no, tell 'em to wait.' Immediately another voice cut in with, 'Track One, auxiliary range Fox – Step one about to strike near Dodge City, Kansas.'

'How near?'

There was no answer. Presently the voice of Track One proper said, 'Impact reported approximately fifteen miles southwest of Dodge City.'

'Casualties?'

Spot One broke in before Track One could answer, 'Step two free, step two free – the ship is now on its own.'

'Mr Coster – *please*, Mr Coster —'

And a totally new voice: 'Spot Two to Blockhouse – we are now tracking the ship. Stand by for reported distances and bearings. Stand by —'

'Track Two to Blockhouse – step four will definitely land in Atlantic, estimated point of impact oh-five-seven miles east of Charleston bearing oh-nine-three. I will repeat —'

Coster looked around irritably. 'Isn't there any drinking-water anywhere in this dump?'

'Mr Coster, please – Palomar says they've just *got* to talk to you.'

Harriman eased over to the door and stepped out. He suddenly felt very much let down, utterly weary, and depressed.

The field looked strange without the ship. He had watched it grow; now suddenly it was gone. The Moon, still rising, seemed oblivious – and space travel was as remote a dream as it had been in his boyhood.

There were several tiny figures prowling around the flash apron where the ship had stood – souvenir hunters, he thought contemptuously. Someone came up to him in the gloom. 'Mr Harriman?'

'Eh?'

'Hopkins – with the AP. How about a statement?'

'Uh? No, no comment. I'm bushed.'

'Oh, now, just a word. How does it feel to have backed the first successful Moon flight – if it is successful?'

'It will be successful.' He thought a moment, then squared his tired shoulders and said, 'Tell them that this is the beginning of the human race's greatest era. Tell them that every one of them will have a chance to follow in Captain LeCroix's footsteps, seek out new planets, wrest a home for themselves in new lands. Tell them that this means new frontiers, a shot in the arm for prosperity. It means —' He ran down. 'That's all tonight. I'm whipped, son. Leave me alone, will you?'

Presently Coster came out, followed by the VIPs. Harriman went up to Coster. 'Everything all right?'

'Sure. Why shouldn't it be? Track three followed him out to the limit of range – all in the groove.' Coster added, 'Step five killed a cow when it grounded.'

'Forget it – we'll have steak for breakfast.' Harriman then had to make conversation with the Governor and the Vice-President, had to escort them out to their ship. Dixon and Entenza left together, less formally; at last Coster and Harriman were alone save for subordinates too junior to constitute a strain and for guards to protect them from the crowds. 'Where you headed, Bob?'

'Up to the Broadmoor and about a week's sleep. How about you?'

'If you don't mind. I'll doss down in your apartment.'

'Help yourself. Sleepy pills in the bathroom.'

'I won't need them.' They had a drink together in Coster's quarters, talked aimlessly, then Coster ordered a copter cab and went to the hotel. Harriman went to bed, got up, read a day-old copy of the Denver *Post* filled with pictures of the *Pioneer*, finally gave up and took two of Coster's sleeping capsules.

10

Someone was shaking him. 'Mr Harriman! Wake up – Mr Coster is on the screen.'

'Huh? Wazza? Oh, all right.' He got up and padded to the phone. Coster was looking tousle-headed and excited. 'Hey, Boss, – *he made it!*'

'Huh? What do you mean?'

'Palomar just called me. They saw his mark and now they've spotted the ship itself. He —'

'Wait a minute, Bob. Slow up. He *can't* be there yet. He

just left last night.'

Coster looked disconcerted. 'What's the matter, Mr Harriman? Don't you feel well? He left Wednesday.'

Vaguely, Harriman began to be oriented. No, the take-off had not been the night before – fuzzily he recalled a drive up into the mountains, a day spent dozing in the sun, some sort of a party at which he had drunk too much. What day was today? He didn't know. If LeCroix had landed on the Moon, then – never mind. 'It's all right, Bob – I was half asleep. I guess I dreamed the take-off all over again. Now tell me the news, slowly.'

Coster started over. 'LeCroix has landed, just west of Archimedes crater. They can see his ship from Palomar. Say, that was a great stunt you thought up, marking the spot with carbon black. Les must have covered two acres with it. They say it shines out like a billboard, through the Big Eye.'

'Maybe we ought to run down and have a look. No – later,' he amended. 'We'll be busy.'

'I don't see what more we can do, Mr Harriman. We've got twelve of our best ballistic computers calculating possible routes for you now.'

Harriman started to tell the man to put on another twelve, switched off the screen instead. He was still at Peterson Field, with one of Skyways' best strato-ships waiting for him outside, waiting to take him to whatever point on the globe LeCroix might ground. LeCroix was in the upper stratosphere, had been there for more than twenty-four hours. The pilot was slowly, cautiously wearing out his terminal velocity, dissipating the incredible kinetic energy as shock wave and radiant heat.

They had tracked him by radar around the globe and around again – and again ... yet there was no way of knowing just where and what sort of landing the pilot would choose to risk. Harriman listened to the running radar reports and cursed the fact that they had elected to save the weight of radio equipment.

The radar figures started coming closer together. The voice broke off and started again: 'He's in his landing glide!'

'Tell the field to get ready!' shouted Harriman. He held his breath and waited. After endless seconds another voice cut in with, 'The Moon-ship is now landing. It will ground somewhere west of Chihuahua in Old Mexico.'

Harriman started for the door at a run.

Coached by radio en route, Harriman's pilot spotted the *Pioneer* incredibly small against the desert sand. He put his own ship quite close to it, in a beautiful landing. Harriman was fumbling at the cabin door before the ship was fairly stopped.

LeCroix was sitting on the ground, resting his back against a skid of his ship and enjoying the shade of its stubby triangular wings. A paisano sheep-herder stood facing him, open-mouthed. As Harriman trotted out and lumbered towards him, LeCroix stood up, flipped a cigarette butt away and said, 'Hi, Boss!'

'Les!' The older man threw his arms around the younger. 'It's good to see you, boy.'

'It's good to see *you*. Pedro here doesn't speak my language.' LeCroix glanced around; there was no one else nearby but the pilot of Harriman's ship. 'Where's the gang? Where's Bob?'

'I didn't wait. They'll surely be along in a few minutes – hey, there they come now!' It was another strato-ship, plunging in to a landing. Harriman turned to his pilot. 'Bill – go over and meet them.'

'Huh? They'll come, never fear.'

'Do as I say.'

'You're the doctor.' The pilot trudged through the sand, his back expressing disapproval. LeCroix looked puzzled. 'Quick, Les – help me with this.'

'This' was the five thousand cancelled envelopes which were supposed to have been to the Moon. They got them out of Harriman's strato-ship and into the Moon-ship, there to be stowed in an empty food-locker, while their actions were still shielded from the later arrivals by the bulk of the strato-ship.

'Whew!' said Harriman. 'That was close. Half a million dollars. We need it, Les.'

'Sure, but look, Mr Harriman, the di —'

'Sssh! The others are coming. How about the other busi-

117

ness? Ready with your act?'

'Yes. But I was trying to tell you —'

'Quiet!'

It was not their colleagues: it was a shipload of reporters, camera-men, mike-men, commentators, technicians. They swarmed over them.

Harriman waved to them jauntily. 'Help yourselves, boys. Get a lot of pictures. Climb through the ship. Make yourselves at home. Look at anything you want to. But go easy on Captain LeCroix – he's tired.'

Another ship had landed, this time with Coster, Dixon, and Strong. Entenza showed up in his own chartered ship and began bossing the TV, pix, and radio-men, in the course of which he almost had a fight with an unauthorized camera crew. A large copter transport grounded and spilled out nearly a platoon of khaki-clad Mexican troops. From somewhere – out of the sand apparently – several dozen native peasants showed up. Harriman broke away from reporters, held a quick and expensive discussion with the captain of the local troops and a degree of order was restored in time to save the *Pioneer* from being picked to pieces.

'Just let that be!' It was LeCroix's voice, from inside the *Pioneer*. Harriman waited and listened. 'None of your business!' the pilot's voice went on, rising higher, 'and put them back!'

Harriman pushed his way to the door of the ship. 'What's the trouble, Les?'

Inside the cramped cabin, hardly large enough for a TV booth, three men stood: LeCroix and two reporters. All three men looked angry. 'What's the trouble, Les?' Harriman repeated. LeCroix was holding a small cloth bag which appeared to be empty. Scattered on the pilot's acceleration rest between him and the reporters were several small, dully brilliant stones. A reporter held one such stone up to the light.

'These guys were poking their noses into things that didn't concern them,' LeCroix said angrily.

The reporter looked at the stone and said, 'You told us to look at what we liked, didn't you, Mr Harriman?'

'Yes.'

'Your pilot here' – he jerked a thumb at LeCroix – 'ap-

118

parently didn't expect us to find these. He had them hidden in the pads of his chair.'

'What of it?'

'They're diamonds.'

'What makes you think so?'

'They're diamonds all right.'

Harriman stopped and unwrapped a cigar. Presently he said, 'Those diamonds were where you found them because I put them there.'

A flashlight went off behind Harriman, a voice said, 'Hold the rock up higher, Jeff.'

The reporter called Jeff obliged, then said, 'That seems an odd thing to do, Mr Harriman.'

'I was interested in the effect of outer space radiations on raw diamonds. On my orders Captain LeCroix placed that sack of diamonds in the ship.'

Jeff whistled thoughtfully. 'You know, Mr Harriman, if you did not have that explanation, I'd think LeCroix had found the rocks on the Moon and was trying to hold out on you.'

'Print that and you will be sued for libel. I have every confidence in Captain LeCroix. Now give me the diamonds.'

Jeff's eyebrows went up. 'But not confidence enough in him to let him keep them, maybe?'

'Give me the stones. Then get out.'

Harriman got LeCroix away from the reporters as quickly as possible and into Harriman's own ship. 'That's all for now,' he told the news and pictures people. 'See us at Peterson Field.'

Once the ship raised ground he turned to LeCroix. 'You did a beautiful job, Les.'

'That reporter named Jeff must be sort of confused.'

'Eh? Oh, *that*. No, I mean the flight. You did it. You're head man on this planet.'

LeCroix shrugged it off. 'Bob built a good ship. It was a cinch. Now about those diamonds —'

'Forget the diamonds. You've done your part. We placed those rocks in the ship; now we tell everybody we did — truthful as can be. It's not our fault if they don't believe us.'

'But, Mr Harriman —'

'What?'

LeCroix unzipped a pocket in his overalls, hauled out a soiled handkerchief, knotted into a bag. He untied it – and spilled into Harriman's hands many more diamonds than had been displayed in the ship – larger, finer diamonds.

Harriman stared at them. He began to chuckle.

Presently he shoved them back at LeCroix. 'Keep them.'

'I figure they belong to all of us.'

'Well, keep them for us, then. And keep your mouth shut about them. No, wait.' He picked out two large stones. 'I'll have rings made from these two, one for you, one for me. But keep your mouth shut, or they won't be worth anything, except as curiosities.'

It was quite true, he thought. Long ago the diamond syndicate had realized that diamonds in plentiful supply were worth little more than glass, except for industrial uses. Earth had more than enough for that, more than enough for jewels. If Moon diamonds were literally 'common as pebbles', then they were just that – pebbles.

Not worth the expense of bringing them to earth.

But now take uranium. If that were plentiful —

Harriman sat back and indulged in day-dreaming.

Presently LeCroix said softly, 'You know, Boss, it's wonderful there.'

'Eh? Where?'

'Why, on the Moon, of course. I'm going back. I'm going back just as soon as I can. We've got to get busy on the new ship.'

'Sure, sure! And this time we'll build one big enough for all of us. This time I go, too!'

'You bet.'

'Les —' The older man spoke almost diffidently. 'What does it look like when you look back and see the Earth?'

'Huh? It looks like – it looks —' LeCroix stopped. 'Hell's bells, Boss, there isn't any way to tell you. It's wonderful, that's all. The sky is black and – well, wait until you see the pictures I took. Better yet, wait and see it yourself.'

Harriman nodded. 'But it's hard to wait.'

11

'FIELDS OF DIAMONDS ON THE MOON!!!'
'BILLIONAIRE BACKER DENIES DIAMOND STORY
   Says Jewels Taken into Space for Science Reasons'
'MOON DIAMONDS; HOAX OR FACT?'
'— but consider this, friends of the invisible audience:
why would anyone take diamonds *to* the moon? Every
ounce of that ship and its cargo was calculated; diamonds
would not be taken along without reason. Many scientific
authorities have pronounced Mr Harriman's professed reason an absurdity. It is easy to guess that diamonds might be
taken along for the purpose of "salting" the Moon, so to
speak, with earthly jewels, with the intention of convincing
us that diamonds exist on the Moon — but Mr Harriman,
his pilot Captain LeCroix, and everyone connected with the
enterprise have sworn from the beginning that the diamonds *did not* come from the Moon. But it is an absolute
certainty that the diamonds were in the space-ship when it
landed. Cut it how you will; this reporter is going to try to
buy some lunar diamonds mining stock —'

Strong was, as usual, already in the office when Harriman came in. Before the partners could speak, the screen
called out, 'Mr Harriman. Rotterdam calling.'
   'Tell them to go plant a tulip.'
   'Mr van der Velde is waiting, Mr Harriman.'
   'Okay.'
   Harriman let the Duchman talk, then said, 'Mr van der
Velde, the statements attributed to me are absolutely cor-
rect. I put those diamonds the reporters saw into the ship
before it took off. They were mined right here on Earth. In
fact I bought them when I came over to see you; I can
prove it.'
   'But, Mr Harriman —'
   'Suit yourself. There may be more diamonds on the
Moon than you can run and jump over. I don't guarantee it.
But I do guarantee that those diamonds the newspapers are
talking about came from Earth.'
   'Mr Harriman, why would you send diamonds to the

Moon? Perhaps you intended to fool us, no?'

'Have it your own way. But I've said all along that those diamonds came from Earth. Now see here: you took an option – an option on an option, so to speak. If you want to make the second payment on that option and keep it in force, the deadline is nine o'clock Thursday, New York time, as specified in the contract. Make up your mind.'

He switched off and found his partner looking at him sourly. 'What's eating you?'

'I wondered about those diamonds, too, Delos. So I've been looking through the weight schedule of the *Pioneer*.'

'Didn't know you were interested in engineering.'

'I can read figures.'

'Well, you found it, didn't you? Schedule F-17-c, two ounces, allocated to me personally.'

'I found it. It sticks out like a sore thumb. But I didn't find something else.'

Harriman felt a cold chill in his stomach. 'What?'

'I didn't find a schedule for the cancelled covers.' Strong stared at him.

'It must be there. Let me see that weight schedule.'

'It's not there, Delos. You know, I thought it was funny when you insisted on going to meet Captain LeCroix by yourself. What happened, Delos? Did you sneak them aboard?' He continued to stare while Harriman fidgeted. 'We've put over some sharp business deals – but this will be the first time that anyone can say that the firm of Harriman and Strong has cheated.'

'Damn it, George – I would cheat, lie, steal, beg, bribe – do *anything* to accomplish what we have accomplished.'

Harriman got up and paced the room. 'We *had* to have that money, or the ship would never have taken off. We're cleaned out. You know that, don't you?'

Strong nodded. 'But those covers should have gone to the Moon. That's what we contracted to do.'

'Damn it, I just forgot it. Then it was too late to figure the weight in. But it doesn't matter. I figured that if the trip was a failure, if LeCroix cracked up, nobody would know or care that the covers hadn't gone. And I knew if he made it, it wouldn't matter; we'd have plenty of money. And we will, George, we will!'

'We've got to pay the money back.'

'Now? Give me time, George. Everybody concerned is happy the way it is. Wait until we recover our stake; then I'll buy every one of those covers back – out of my own pocket. That's a promise.'

Strong continued to sit. Harriman stopped in front of him. 'I ask you, George, is it worth while to wreck an enterprise of this size for a purely theoretical point?'

Strong sighed and said, 'When the time comes, use the firm's money.'

'That's the spirit! But I'll use my own, I promise you.'

'No, the firm's money. If we're in it together, we're in it together.'

'OK, if that's the way you want it.'

Harriman turned back to his desk. Neither of the two partners had anything to say for a long while. Presently Dixon and Entenza were announced.

'Well, Jack,' said Harriman. 'Feel better now?'

'No, thanks to you. I had to fight for what I did put on the air – and some of it was pirated as it was, Delos, there should have been a television pick-up in the ship.'

'Don't fret about it. As I told you, we couldn't spare the weight this time. But there will be the next trip, and the next. Your concession is going to be worth a pile of money.'

Dixon cleared his throat. 'That's what we came to see you about, Delos. What are your plans?'

'Plans? We go right ahead. Les and Coster and I make the next trip. We set up a permanent base. Maybe Coster stays behind. The third trip we send a real colony – nuclear engineers, miners, hydroponics experts, communications engineers. We'll found Luna City, first city of another planet.'

Dixon looked thoughtful. 'And when does this begin to pay off?'

'What do you mean by "pay off"? Do you want your capital back, or do you want to begin to see some return on your investment? I can cut it either way.'

Entenza was about to say that he wanted his investment back; Dixon cut in first, 'Profits, naturally. The investment is already made.'

'Fine!'

'But I don't see how you expect profits. Certainly, Le-Croix made the trip and got back safely. There is honour for all of us. But where are the royalties?'

'Give the crop time to ripen, Dan. Do I look worried? What are our assets?' Harriman ticked them off on his fingers. 'Royalties on pictures, television, radio —'

'Those things go to Jack.'

'Take a look at the agreement. He has the concession, but he pays the firm – that's all of us – for them.'

Dixon said, 'Shut up, Jack!' before Entenza could speak, then added, 'What else? That won't pull us out of the red.'

'Endorsements galore. Monty's boys are working on that. Royalties from the greatest best-seller yet – I've got a ghost writer and a stenographer following LeCroix around this very minute. A franchise for the first and only space line —'

'From whom?'

'We'll get it. Kamens and Montgomery are in Paris now, working on it. I'm joining them this afternoon. And we'll tie down that franchise with a franchise from *the other end*, just as soon as we can get a permanent colony there, no matter how small. It will be the autonomous state of Luna, under the protection of the United Nations – and no ship will land or take off in its territory without its permission. Besides that we'll have the right to franchise a dozen other companies for various purposes – and tax them, too – just as soon as we set up the Municipal Corporation of the City of Luna under the laws of the State of Luna. We'll sell everything but vacuum – we'll even sell vacuum, for experimental purposes. And don't forget, we'll still have a big chunk of real estate, sovereign title in us – as a state – and not yet sold. The Moon is *big*.'

'Your ideas are rather big, too, Delos,' Dixon said drily. 'But what actually happens next?'

'First we get the title confirmed by the UN. The Security Council is now in secret session; the Assembly meets to-night. Things will be popping; that's why I've got to be there. When the United Nations decides – as it will! – that its own non-profit corporation has the only real claim to the Moon, then I get busy. The poor little weak non-profit corporation is going to grant a number of things to some real honest-to-god corporations with hair on their chests –

in return for help in setting up a physics research lab, an astronomical observatory, a lunography institute, and some other perfectly proper non-profit enterprises. That's our interim pitch until we get a permanent colony with its own laws. Then we —'

Dixon gestured impatiently. 'Never mind the legal shenanigans, Delos. I've known you long enough to know that you can figure out such angles. What do we actually have to *do* next?'

'Huh? We've got to build another ship, a bigger one. Not actually bigger, but effectively bigger. Coster has started the design of a surface catapult – it will reach from Manitou Springs to the top of Pikes Peak. With it we can put a ship in free orbit around the Earth. Then we'll use such a ship to fuel more ships – it amounts to a space station, like the power station. It adds up to a way to get there on chemical power without having to throw away nine-tenths of your ship to do it.'

'Sounds expensive.'

'It will be. But don't worry; we've got a couple of dozen piddling little things to keep the money coming in while we get set up on a commercial basis, then we sell stock. We sold stock before; now we'll sell a thousand dollars' worth where we sold ten before.'

'And you think that will carry you through until the enterprise as a whole is on a paying basis? Face it, Delos, the thing as a whole doesn't pay off until you have ships plying between here and the Moon on a paying basis, figured in freight and passenger charges. That means customers, with cash. What is there on the Moon to ship – and who pays for it?'

'Dan, don't you believe there will be? If not, why are you here?'

'I believe in it, Delos – or I believe in you. But what's your time schedule? What's your budget? What's your prospective commodity? And please don't mention diamonds; I think I understand that caper.'

Harriman chewed his cigar for a few moments. 'There's one valuable commodity we'll start shipping at once.'

'What?'

'Knowledge.'

Entenza snorted. Strong looked puzzled. Dixon nodded. 'I'll buy that. Knowledge is always worth something – to the man who knows how to exploit it. And I'll agree that the Moon is a place to find new knowledge. I'll assume that you can make the next trip pay off. What's your budget and your time-table for that?'

Harriman did not answer. Strong searched his face closely. To him Harriman's poker face was as revealing as large print – he decided that his partner had been crowded into a corner. He waited, nervous but ready to back Harriman's play. Dixon went on, 'From the way you describe it, Delos, I judge that you don't have money enough for your next step – and you don't know where you will get it. I believe in you, Delos – and I told you at the start that I did not believe in letting a new business die of anaemia. I'm ready to buy in with a fifth share.'

Harriman stared. 'Look,' he said bluntly, 'you own Jack's share now, don't you?'

'I wouldn't say that.'

'You vote it. It sticks out all over.'

Entenza said, 'That's not true. I'm independent. I —'

'Jack, you're a damn liar,' Harriman said dispassionately. 'Dan, you've got fifty per cent now. Under the present rules I decide deadlocks, which gives me control as long as George sticks by me. If we sell you another share, you vote three-fifths – and are boss. Is that the deal you are looking for?'

'Delos, as I told you. I have confidence in you.'

'But you'd feel happier with the whip hand. Well, I won't do it. I'll let space travel – *real* space travel, with established runs – wait another twenty years before I'll turn loose. I'll let us all go broke and let us live on glory before I'll turn loose. You'll have to think up another scheme.'

Dixon said nothing. Harriman got up and began to pace. He stopped in front of Dixon. 'Dan, if you really understood what this is all about, I'd let you have control. But you don't. You see this as just another way to money and to power. I'm perfectly willing to let you vultures get rich – but I keep control. I'm going to see this thing developed, not milked. The human race is heading out to the stars – and this adventure is going to present new problems com-

126

pared with which atomic power was a kid's toy. The race is about as prepared for it as an innocent virgin is prepared for sex. Unless the whole matter is handled carefully, it will be bitched up. *You*'ll bitch it up, Dan, if I let you have the deciding vote in it – because you don't understand it.'

He caught his breath and went on, 'Take safety, for instance. Do you know *why* I let LeCroix take that ship out instead of taking it myself? Do you think I was afraid? No! I wanted it to come back – *safely*. I didn't want space travel getting another setback. Do you know why we have to have a monopoly, for a few years at least? Because every so-and-so and his brother is going to want to build a Moonship, now that they know it can be done. Remember the first days of ocean flying? After Lindbergh did it every so-called pilot who could lay hands on a crate took off for some over-water point. Some of them even took their kids along. And most of them landed in the drink. Airplanes got a reputation for being dangerous. A few years after that the airlines got so hungry for quick money in a highly competitive field that you couldn't pick up a paper without seeing headlines about another air liner crash.

'That's not going to happen to space travel! I'm not going to let it happen. Space-ships are too big and too expensive; if they get a reputation for being unsafe as well, we might as well have stayed in bed. I run things.'

He stopped.

Dixon waited and then said, 'I said I believed in you, Delos. How much money do you need?'

'Eh? On what terms?'

'Your note.'

'My note? Did you say *my note*?'

'I'd want security, of course.'

Harriman swore. 'I knew there was a hitch in it. Dan, you know damn well everything I've got is tied up in this venture.'

'You have insurance. You have quite a lot of insurance, I know.'

'Yes, but that's all made out to my wife.'

'I seem to have heard you say something about that sort of thing to Jack Entenza,' Dixon said, 'Come now – if I know your tax-happy sort, you have at least one irrevoc-

127

able trust, or paid-up annuities, or something, to keep Mrs Harriman out of the poor house.'

Harriman thought fiercely about it. 'When's the call date on this note?'

'In the sweet bye and bye. I want a no-bankruptcy clause, of course.'

'Why? Such a clause has no legal validity.'

'It would be valid with *you*, wouldn't it?'

'Mmm ... yes. Yes, it would.'

'Then get out your policies and see how big a note you can write.'

Harriman looked at him, turned abruptly and went to his safe. He came back with quite a stack of long, stiff folders. They added them up together; it was an amazingly large sum – for those days. Dixon then consulted a memorandum taken from his pocket and said, 'One seems to be missing – a rather large one. A North Atlantic Mutual policy, I think.'

Harriman glared at him. 'Damn you, am I going to have to fire every confidential clerk in my force?'

'No,' Dixon said mildly, 'I don't get my information from your staff.'

Harriman went back to the safe, got the policy and added it to the pile. Strong spoke up, 'Do you want mine, Mr Dixon?'

'No,' answered Dixon, 'that won't be necessary.' He started stuffing the policies in his pocket. 'I'll keep these, Delos, and attend to keeping up the premiums. I'll bill you, of course. You can send the note and the change-of-beneficiary forms to my office. Here's your draft.' He took out another slip of paper; it was the draft – already made out in the amount of the policies.

Harriman looked at it. 'Sometimes,' he said slowly, 'I wonder who's kidding who?' He tossed the draft over to Strong. 'OK, George, take care of it. I'm off to Paris, boys. Wish me luck.' He strode out as jauntily as a fox-terrier.

Strong looked from the closed door to Dixon, then at the note. 'I ought to tear this thing up!'

'Don't do it,' advised Dixon. 'You see, I really do believe in him.' He added, 'Ever read Carl Sandburg, George?'

'I'm not much of a reader.'

'Try him some time. He tells a story about a man who started a rumour that they had struck oil in hell. Pretty soon everybody has left for hell, to get in on the boom. The man who started the rumour watches them all go, then scratches his head and says to himself that there just *might* be something in it, after all. So he left for hell, too.'

Strong waited, finally he said, 'I don't get the point.'

'The point is that I just want to be ready to protect myself if necessary, George – and so should you. Delos might begin believing his own rumours. Diamonds! Come, Jack.'

12

The ensuing months were as busy as the period before the flight of the *Pioneer* (now honourably retired to the Smithsonian Institution). One engineering staff and great gangs of men were working on the catapult; two more staffs were busy with two new ships – the *Mayflower*, and the *Colonial*; a third ship was on the drafting tables. Ferguson was chief engineer for all of this; Coster, still buffered by Jock Berkeley, was engineering consultant, working where and as he chose. Colorado Springs was a boom town; the Denver–Trinidad roadcity settlements spread out at the Springs until they surrounded Peterson Field.

Harriman was as busy as a cat with two tails. The constantly expanding exploitation and promotion took eight full days a week of his time, but, by working Kamens and Montgomery almost to ulcers and by doing without sleep himself, he created frequent opportunities to run out to Colorado and talk things over with Coster.

Luna City, it was decided, would be founded on the very next trip. The *Mayflower* was planned for a pay-load not only of seven passengers, but with air, water, and food to carry four of them over to the next trip; they would live in an aluminium Quonset-type hut, sealed, pressurized, and buried under the loose soil of Luna until – and assuming – they were succoured.

The choice of the four extra passengers gave rise to another contest, another publicity exploitation – and more sale of stock. Harriman insisted that they be two married couples, over the united objections of scientific organizations everywhere. He gave in only to the extent of agreeing that there was no objection to all four being scientists, providing they constituted two married couples. This gave rise to several hasty marriages – and some divorces, after the choices were announced.

The *Mayflower* was the maximum size that calculations showed would be capable of getting into free orbit around the Earth from the boost of the catapult, plus the blast of her own engines. Before she took off, four other ships, quite as large, would precede her. But they were not space-ships; they were mere tankers – nameless. The most finicky of ballistic calculations, the most precise of launchings, would place them in the same orbit at the same spot. There the *Mayflower* would rendezvous and accept their remaining fuel.

This was the trickiest part of the entire project. If the four tankers could be placed close enough together, Le-Croix, using a tiny manoeuvring reserve, could bring his new ship to them. If not – well, it gets very lonely out in space.

Serious thought was given to placing pilots in the tankers and accepting as a penalty the use of enough fuel from one tanker to permit a get-away boat, a lifeboat with wings, to decelerate, reach the atmosphere and brake to a landing. Coster found a cheaper way.

A radar pilot, whose ancestor was the proximity fuse and whose immediate parents could be found in the homing devices of guided missiles, was given the task of bringing the tankers together. The first tanker would not be so equipped, but the second tanker through its robot would smell out the first and home on it with a pint-sized rocket engine, using the smallest of vectors to bring them together. The third would home on the first two and the fourth on the group.

LeCroix should have no trouble – if the scheme worked.

13

Strong wanted to show Harriman the sales reports on the H & S automatic household switch; Harriman brushed them aside.

Strong shoved them back under his nose. 'You'd better start taking an interest in such things, Delos. *Somebody* around this office had better start seeing to it that some money comes in – some money that belongs to us, personally – or you'll be selling apples on a street corner.'

Harriman leaned back and clasped his hands back of his head. 'George, how can you talk that way on a day like this? Is there no poetry in your soul? Didn't you hear what I said when I came in? *The rendezvous worked*. Tankers one and two are as close together as Siamese twins. We'll be leaving within the week.'

'That's as may be. Business has to go on.'

'You keep it going; I've got a date. When did Dixon say he would be over?'

'He's due now.'

'Good!' Harriman bit the end off a cigar and went on, 'You know, George, I'm not sorry I didn't get to make the first trip. Now I've still got it to do. I'm as expectant as a bridegroom – and as happy.' He started to hum.

Dixon came in without Entenza, a situation that had obtained since the day Dixon had dropped the pretence that he controlled only one share. He shook hands. 'You heard the news, Dan?'

'George told me.'

'This is it – or almost. A week from now, more or less, I'll be on the Moon. I can hardly believe it.'

Dixon sat down silently. Harriman went on, 'Aren't you even going to congratulate me? Man, this is a great day!'

Dixon said, 'D. D., why are you going?'

'Huh? Don't ask foolish questions. This is what I have been working towards.'

'It's not a foolish question. I asked why *you* were going. The four colonists have an obvious reason, and each is a selected specialist observer as well. LeCroix is the pilot. Coster is the man who is designing the permanent colony. But why are *you* going? What's your function?'

'My function? Why, I'm the guy who runs things. Shucks, I'm going to run for mayor when I get there. Have a cigar, friend – the name's Harriman. Don't forget to vote.' He grinned.

Dixon did not smile. 'I did not know you planned on staying.'

Harriman looked sheepish. 'Well, that's still up in the air. If we get the shelter built in a hurry, we may save enough in the way of supplies to let me sort of lay over until the next trip. You wouldn't begrudge me that, would you?'

Dixon looked him in the eye. 'Delos, I can't let you go at all.'

Harriman was too startled to talk at first. At last he managed to say, 'Don't joke, Dan. I'm going. You can't stop me. Nothing on Earth can stop me.'

Dixon shook his head. 'I can't permit it, Delos. I've got too much sunk in this. If you go and anything happens to you, I lose it all.'

'That's silly. You and George would just carry on, that's all.'

'Ask George.'

Strong had nothing to say. He did not seem anxious to meet Harriman's eyes. Dixon went on, 'Don't try to kid your way out of it, Delos. This venture is you, and you are this venture. If you get killed, the whole thing folds up. I don't say space travel folds up; I think you've already given that a boost that will carry it along even with lesser men in your shoes. But as for this venture – our Company – it will fold up. George and I will have to liquidate at about half a cent on the dollar. It would take sale of patent rights to get that much. The tangible assets aren't worth anything.'

'Damn it, it's the intangibles we sell. You knew that all along.'

'You are the intangible asset, Delos. You are the goose that lays the golden eggs. I want you to stick around until you've laid them. You must not risk your neck in space flight until you have this thing on a profit-making basis, so that any competent manager, such as George or myself, thereafter can keep it solvent. I mean it, Delos. I've got too much in it to see you risk it in a joy ride.'

Harriman stood up and pressed his fingers down on the edge of his desk. He was breathing hard. 'You can't stop me!' he said slowly and forcefully. 'You knew all along that I meant to go. You can't stop me now. Not all the forces of heaven or hell can stop me.'

Dixon answered quietly, 'I'm sorry, Delos. But I can stop you and I will. I can tie up that ship out there.'

'Try it! I own as many lawyers as you do – and better ones!'

'I think you will find that you are not as popular in American courts as you once were – not since the United States found out it didn't own the Moon, after all.'

'Try it, I tell you. I'll break you, and I'll take your shares away from you, too.'

'Easy, Delos! I've no doubt you have some scheme whereby you could milk the basic Company right away from George and me if you decided to. But it won't be necessary. Nor will it be necessary to tie up the ship. I want that flight to take place as much as you do. But you won't be on it, because you will decide not to go.'

'I will, eh? Do I look crazy from where you sit?'

'No, on the contrary.'

'Then why won't I go?'

'Because of your note that I hold. I want to collect it.'

'What? There's no due date.'

'No. But I want to be sure to collect it.'

'Why, you dumb fool, if I get killed you collect it sooner than ever.'

'Do I? You are mistaken, Delos. If you are killed – on a flight to the Moon – I collect nothing. I know; I've checked with every one of the companies underwriting you. Most of them have escape clauses covering experimental vehicles that date back to early aviation. In any case, all of them will cancel and fight it out in court if you set foot inside that ship.'

'You put them up to this!'

'Calm down, Delos. You'll be bursting a blood vessel. Certainly I queried them, but I was legitimately looking after my own interests. I don't want to collect on that note – not now, not by your death. I want you to pay it back out of your own earnings, by staying here and nursing this Company through till it's stable.'

Harriman chucked his cigar, almost unsmoked and badly chewed, at a waste-basket. He missed. 'I don't give a hoot if you lose on it. If you hadn't stirred them up, they'd have paid without a quiver.'

133

'But it did dig up a weak point in your plans, Delos. If space travel is to be a success, insurance will have to reach out and cover the insured anywhere.'

'Damn it, one of them does now – N. A. Mutual.'

'I've seen their ad and I've looked over what they claim to offer. It's just window-dressing, with the usual escape clause. No, insurance will have to be revamped, all sorts of insurance.'

Harriman looked thoughtful. 'I'll look into it. George, call Kamens. Maybe we'll have to float our own Company.'

'Never mind Kamens,' objected Dixon. 'The point is you can't go on this trip. You have too many details of that sort to watch and plan for and nurse along.'

Harriman looked back at him. 'You haven't got it through your head, Dan, that I'm going! Tie up the ship if you can. If you put sheriffs around it, I'll have goons there to toss them aside.'

Dixon looked pained. 'I hate to mention this point, Delos, but I am afraid you will be stopped even if I drop dead.'

'How?'

'Your wife.'

'What's she got to do with it?'

'She's ready to sue for separate maintenance right now – she's found out about this insurance thing. When she hears about this present plan she'll force you into court and force an accounting of your assets.'

'*You put her up to it!*'

Dixon hesitated. He knew that Entenza had spilled the beans to Mrs Harriman – maliciously. Yet there seemed no point in adding to a personal feud. 'She's bright enough to have done some investigating on her own account. I won't deny I've talked to her – but she sent for me.'

'I'll fight both of you!' Harriman stomped to a window, stood looking out – it was a real window; he liked to look at the sky.

Dixon came over and put a hand on his shoulder, saying softly, 'Don't take it this way, Delos. Nobody's trying to keep you from your dream. But you can't go just yet; you can't let us down. We've stuck with you this far; you owe it to us to stick with us until it's done.'

134

Harriman did not answer; Dixon went on, 'If you don't feel any loyalty towards me, how about George? He's stuck with you *against* me, when it hurt him, when he thought you were ruining him – and you surely were, unless you finish this job. How about George, Delos? Are you going to let him down, too?'

Harriman swung around, ignoring Dixon and facing Strong. 'What about it, George? Do you think I should stay behind?'

Strong rubbed his hands and chewed his lip. Finally he looked up. 'It's all right with me, Delos. You do what you think is best.'

Harriman stood looking at him for a long moment, his face working as if he were going to cry. Then he said huskily: 'Okay, you bastards. Okay. I'll stay behind.'

14

It was one of those glorious evenings so common in the Pikes Peak region after a day in which the sky has been well scrubbed by thunderstorms. The track of the catapult crawled in a straight line up the face of the mountain, whole shoulders having been carved away to permit it. At the temporary space port, still raw from construction, Harriman, in company with visiting notables, was saying goodbye to the passengers and crew of the *Mayflower*.

The crowds came right up to the rail of the catapult. There was no need to keep them back from the ship; the jets would not blast until she was high over the peak. Only the ship itself was guarded, the ship and the gleaming rails.

Dixon and Strong, together for company and mutual support, hung back at the edge of the area roped off for passengers and officials. They watched Harriman jollying those about to leave: 'Good-bye, Doctor. Keep an eye on him, Janet. Don't let him go looking for Moon Maidens.' They saw him engage Coster in private conversation, then clap the younger man on the back.

'Keeps his chin up, doesn't he?' whispered Dixon.

'Maybe we should have let him go,' answered Strong.

'Eh? Nonsense! We've got to have him. Anyway, his

135

place in history is secure.'

'He doesn't care about history,' Strong answered seriously, 'he just wants to go to the Moon.'

'Well, confound it – he can go to the Moon ... as soon as he gets his job done. After all, it's his job. He made it.'

'I know.'

Harriman turned around, saw them, started towards them. They shut up. 'Don't duck,' he said jovially. 'It's all right. I'll go on the next trip. By then I plan to have it running itself. You'll see.' He turned back towards the *Mayflower*. 'Quite a sight, isn't she?'

The outer door was closed; ready lights winked along the track and from the control tower. A siren sounded.

Harriman moved a step or two closer.

'There she goes!'

It was a shout from the whole crowd. The great ship started slowly, softly up the track, gathered speed, and shot towards the distant peak. She was already tiny by the time she curved up the face and burst into the sky.

She hung there a split second, then a plume of light exploded from her tail. Her jets had fired.

Then she was a shining light in the sky, a ball of flame, then – nothing. She was gone, upward and outward, to her rendezvous with her tankers.

The crowd had pushed to the west end of the platform as the ship swarmed up the mountain. Harriman had stayed where he was, nor had Dixon and Strong followed the crowd. The three were alone. Harriman most alone, for he did not seem aware that the others were near him. He was watching the sky.

Strong was watching him. Presently Strong barely whispered to Dixon, 'Do you read the Bible?'

'Some.'

'He looks as Moses must have looked when he gazed out over the Promised Land.'

Harriman dropped his eyes from the sky and saw them. 'You guys still here?' he said. 'Come on – there's work to be done.'

'—ALL YOU ZOMBIES—'

2217 Time Zone V (EST) 7 Nov 1970 NYC – 'Pop's Place': I was polishing a brandy snifter when the Unmarried Mother came in. I noted the time – 10.17 p.m. zone five or eastern time 7 November 1970. Temporal agents always notice time & date; we must.

The Unmarried Mother was a man twenty-five years old, no taller than I am, immature features, and a touchy temper. I didn't like his looks – I never had – but he was a lad I was here to recruit, he was my boy. I gave him my best barkeep's smile.

Maybe I'm too critical. He wasn't swish; his nickname came from what he always said when some nosy type asked him his line: 'I'm an unmarried mother.' If he felt less than murderous he would add: '– at four cents a word. I write confession stories.'

If he felt nasty, he would wait for somebody to make something of it. He had a lethal style of in-fighting, like a female cop – one reason I wanted him. Not the only one.

He had a load on and his face showed that he despised people more than usual. Silently I poured a double shot of Old Underwear and left the bottle. He drank, poured another.

I wiped the bar top. 'How's the "Unmarried Mother" racket?'

His fingers tightened on the glass and he seemed about to throw it at me; I felt for the sap under the bar. In temporal manipulation you try to figure everything, but there are so many factors that you never take needless risks.

I saw him relax that tiny amount they teach you to watch for in the Bureau's training school. 'Sorry,' I said. 'Just asking, "How's business?" Make it "How's the weather?" '

He looked sour. 'Business is okay. I write 'em, they print 'em, I eat.'

I poured myself one, leaned towards him. 'Matter of fact,' I said, 'you write a nice stick – I've sampled a few.

137

You have an amazingly sure touch with the woman's angle.'

It was a slip I had to risk; he never admitted what pen-names he used. But he was boiled enough to pick up only the last. ' "Woman's angle!" ' he repeated with a snort. 'Yeah, I know the woman's angle. I should.'

'So?' I said doubtfully. 'Sisters?'

'No. You wouldn't believe me if I told you.'

'Now, now,' I answered mildly, 'bartenders and psychia-trists learn that nothing is stranger than the truth. Why, son, if you heard the stories I do – well, you'd make your-self rich. Incredible.'

'You don't know what "incredible" means!'

'So? Nothing astonishes me. I've always heard worse.'

He snorted again. 'Want to bet the rest of the bottle?'

'I'll bet a full bottle.' I placed one on the bar.

'Well –' I signalled to my other bartender to handle the trade. We were at the far end, a single stool space that I kept private by loading the bar top by it with jars of pickled eggs and other clutter. A few were at the other end watch-ing the fights and somebody was playing the juke box – private as a bed where we were. 'Okay,' he began, 'to start with, I'm a bastard.'

'No distinction around here,' I said.

'I mean it,' he snapped. 'My parents weren't married.'

'Still no distinction,' I insisted. 'Neither were mine.'

'When —' He stopped, gave me the first warm look I ever saw on him. 'You mean that?'

'I do. A one-hundred-percent bastard. In fact,' I added, 'No one in my family ever marries. All bastards.'

'Don't try to top me – *you're* married.' He pointed at my ring.

'Oh, that.' I showed it to him. 'It just looks like a wed-ding ring; I wear it to keep women off.' That ring is an antique I bought in 1985 from a fellow operative – he had fetched it from pre-Christian Crete. 'The Worm Ouroboros ... the World Snake that eats its own tail, forever without end. A symbol of the Great Paradox.'

He barely glanced at it. 'If you're really a bastard, you know how it feels. When I was a little girl —'

'Wups!' I said. 'Did I hear you correctly?'

'Who's telling this story? When I was a little girl – Look,

138

ever hear of Christine Jorgenson? Or Roberta Cowell?'

'Uh, sex change cases? You're trying to tell me —'

'Don't interrupt or swelp me, I won't talk. I was a foundling, left in an orphanage in Cleveland in 1945 when I was a month old. When I was a little girl, I envied kids with parents. Then, when I learned about sex – and believe me, Pop, you learn fast in an orphanage —'

'I know.'

'– I made a solemn vow that any kid of mine would have both a pop and a mom. It kept me "pure", quite a feat in that vicinity – I had to learn to fight to manage it. Then I got older and realized I stood darned little chance of getting married – for the same reason I hadn't been adopted.' He scowled. 'I was horse-faced and buck-toothed, flat-chested and straight-haired.'

'You don't look any worse than I do.'

'Who cares how a barkeep looks? Or a writer? But people wanting to adopt pick little blue-eyed golden-haired morons. Later on, the boys want bulging breasts, a cute face, and an Oh-you-wonderful-male manner.' He shrugged. 'I couldn't compete. So I decided to join the W.E.N.C.H.E.S.'

'Eh?'

'Women's Emergency National Corps, Hospitality & Entertainment Section, what they now call "Space Angels" – Auxiliary Nursing Group, Extraterrestrial Legions.'

I knew both terms, once I had them chronized. Although we now use still a third name; it's that *élite* military service corps: Women's Hospitality Order Refortifying & Encouraging Spacemen. Vocabulary shift is the worst hurdle in time-jumps – did you know that 'service station' once meant a dispensary for petroleum fractions? Once on an assignment in the Churchill Era a woman said to me, 'Meet me at the service station next door' – which is *not* what it sounds; a 'service station' (then) wouldn't have a bed in it.

He went on: 'It was when they first admitted you can't send men into space for months and years and not relieve the tension. You remember how the wowsers screamed? – that improved my chances, volunteers were scarce. A gal had to be respectable, preferably virgin (they liked to train

139

them from scratch), above average mentally, and stable emotionally, But most volunteers were old hookers, or neurotics who would crack up ten days off Earth. So I didn't need looks; if they accepted me, they would fix my buck teeth, put a wave in my hair, teach me to walk and dance and how to listen to a man pleasingly, and everything else – plus training for the prime duties. They would even use plastic surgery if it would help – nothing too good for Our Boys.

'Best yet, they made sure you didn't get pregnant during your enlistment – and you were almost certain to marry at the end of your hitch. Same way today, A.N.G.E.L.S. marry spacers – they talk the language.

'When I was eighteen I was placed as a "mother's helper". This family simply wanted a cheap servant but I didn't mind as I couldn't enlist till I was twenty-one. I did housework and went to night school – pretending to continue my high school typing and shorthand but going to a charm class instead, to better my chances for enlistment.

'Then I met this city slicker with his hundred dollar bills.' He scowled. 'The no-good actually did have a wad of hundred-dollar bills. He showed me one night, told me to help myself.

'But I didn't. I liked him. He was the first man I ever met who was nice to me without trying to take my pants off. I quit night school to see him oftener. It was the happiest time of my life.

'Then one night in the park my pants did come off.'

He stopped. I said, 'And then?'

'And then *nothing*! I never saw him again. He walked me home and told me he loved me – and kissed me goodnight and never came back.' He looked grim. 'If I could find him, I'd kill him!'

'Well,' I sympathized, 'I know how you feel. But killing him – just for doing what comes naturally – hmm ... Did you struggle?'

'Huh? What's that got to do with it?'

'Quite a bit. Maybe he deserves a couple of broken arms for running out on you, but —'

'He deserves worse than that! Wait till you hear. Somehow I kept anyone from suspecting and decided it was all

140

for the best. I hadn't really loved him and probably would never love anybody – and I was more eager to join the W.E.N.C.H.E.S. than ever. I wasn't disqualified, they didn't insist on virgins. I cheered up.

'It wasn't until my skirts got tight that I realized.'

'Pregnant?'

'The bastard had me higher'n a kite! Those skinflints I lived with ignored it as long as I could work – then kicked me out and the orphanage wouldn't take me back. I landed in a charity ward surrounded by other big bellies and trotted bedpans until my time came.

'One night I found myself on an operating-table, with a nurse saying, "Relax. Now breathe deeply."'

'I woke up in bed, numb from the chest down. My surgeon came in. "How do you feel?" he says cheerfully.

' "Like a mummy."

' "Naturally. You're wrapped like one and full of dope to keep you numb. You'll get well – but a Caesarian isn't a hangnail."

' "Caesarian?" I said. "Doc – *did I lose the baby?*"

' "Oh, no. Your baby's fine."

' "Oh. Boy or girl?"

' "A healthy little girl. Five pounds, three ounces."

'I relaxed. It's something, to have made a baby. I told myself I would go somewhere and tack "Mrs" on my name and let the kid think her papa was dead – no orphanage for *my* kid!

'But the surgeon was talking. "Tell me, uh—" He avoided my name. "– did you ever think your glandular set-up was odd?'

'I said, "Huh? Of course not. What are you driving at?'

'He hesitated. "I'll give you this in one dose, then a hypo to let you sleep off your jitters. You'll have 'em."

' "Why?" I demanded.

' "Ever hear of that Scottish physician who was female until she was thirty-five? – then had surgery and became legally and medically a man? Got married. All okay."

' "What's that got to do with me?"

' "That's what I'm saying. You're a man."

'I tried to sit up. "*What?*"

' "Take it easy. When I opened you, I found a mess. I

141

sent for the Chief of Surgery while I got the baby out, then we held a consultation with you on the table – and worked for hours to salvage what we could. You had two full sets of organs, both immature, but with the female set well enough developed that you had a baby. They could never be any use to you again, so we took them out and re-arranged things so that you can develop properly as a man." He put a hand on me. "Don't worry. You're young, your bones will readjust, we'll watch your glandular balance – and make a fine young man out of you."

'I started to cry. "What about my *baby*?"

' "Well, you can't nurse her, you haven't milk enough for a kitten. If I were you, I wouldn't see her – put her up for adoption."

' "*No!*"

'He shrugged. "The choice is yours; you're her mother – well, her parent. But don't worry now; we'll get you well first."

'Next day they let me see the kid and I saw her daily – trying to get used to her. I had never seen a brand-new baby and had no idea how awful they look – my daughter looked like an orange monkey. My feeling changed to cold determination to do right by her. But four weeks later that didn't mean anything.'

'Eh?'

'She was snatched.'

' "Snatched?" '

The Unmarried Mother almost knocked over the bottle we had bet. 'Kidnapped – stolen from the hospital nursery!' He breathed hard. 'How's that for taking the last thing a man's got to live for?'

'A bad deal,' I agreed. 'Let's pour you another. No clues?'

'Nothing the police could trace. Somebody came to see her, claimed to be her uncle. While the nurse had her back turned, he walked out with her.'

'Description?'

'Just a man, with a face-shaped face, like yours or mine.' He frowned. 'I think it was the baby's father. The nurse swore it was an older man but he probably used make-up. Who else would swipe my baby? Childless women pull

142

such stunts – but whoever heard of a man doing it?'

'What happened to you then?'

'Eleven more months of that grim place and three operations. In four months I started to grow a beard; before I was out I was shaving regularly ... and no longer doubted that I was male.' He grinned wryly. 'I was staring down nurses' necklines.'

'Well,' I said, 'seems to me you came through okay. Here you are, a normal man, making good money, no real troubles. And the life of a female is not an easy one.'

He glared at me. 'A lot you know about it!'

'So?'

'Ever hear the expression "a ruined woman"?'

'Mmm, years ago. Doesn't mean much today.'

'I was as ruined as a woman can be; that bastard *really* ruined me – I was no longer a woman ... and I didn't know *how* to be a man.'

'Takes getting used to, I suppose.'

'You have no idea. I don't mean learning how to dress, or not walking into the wrong rest-room; I learned those in the hospital. But how could I *live*? What job could I get? Hell, I couldn't even drive a car. I didn't know a trade; I couldn't do manual labour – too much scar tissue, too tender.

'I hated him for having ruined me for the W.E.N.C.H.E.S., too, but I didn't know how much until I tried to join the Space Corps instead. One look at my belly and I was marked unfit for military service. The medical officer spent time on me just from curiosity; he had read about my case.

'So I changed my name and came to New York. I got by as a fry cook, then rented a typewriter and set myself up as a public stenographer – what a laugh! In four months I typed four letters and one manuscript. The manuscript was for *Real Life Tales* and a waste of paper, but the goof who wrote it, sold it. Which gave me an idea; I bought a stack of confession magazines and studied them.' He looked cynical. 'Now you know how I get the authentic woman's angle on an unmarried mother story ... through the only version I haven't sold – the true one. Do I win the bottle?'

I pushed it towards him. I was upset myself, but there was work to do. I said, 'Son, you still want to lay hands on

143

that so-and-so?'

His eyes lighted up – a feral gleam.

'Hold it!' I said. 'You wouldn't kill him?'

He chuckled nastily. 'Try me.'

'Take it easy. I know more about it than you think I do. I can help you. I know where he is.'

He reached across the bar. *'Where is he?'*

I said softly, 'Let go my shirt, sonny – or you'll land in the alley and we'll tell the cops you fainted.' I showed him the sap.

He let go. 'Sorry. But where is he?' He looked at me. 'And how do you know so much?'

'All in good time. There are records – hospital records, orphanage records, medical records. The matron of your orphanage was Mrs Fetherage – right? She was followed by Mrs Gruenstein – right? Your name, as a girl, was "Jane" – right? And you didn't tell me any of this – right?'

I had him baffled and a bit scared. 'What's this? You trying to make trouble for me?'

'No indeed. I've your welfare at heart. I can put this character in your lap. You do to him as you see fit – and I guarantee that you'll get away with it. But I don't think you'll kill him. You'd be nuts to – and you aren't nuts. Not quite.'

He brushed it aside. 'Cut the noise. *Where is he?'*

I poured him a short one; he was drunk but anger was offsetting it. 'Not so fast. I do something for you – you do something for me.'

'Uh ... what?'

'You don't like your work. What would you say to high pay, steady work, unlimited expense account, your own boss on the job, and lots of variety and adventure?'

He stared. 'I'd say, "Get those goddam reindeer off my roof!" Shove it, Pop – there's no such job.'

'Okay, put it this way: I hand him to you, you settle with him, then try my job. If it's not all I claim – well, I can't hold you.'

He was wavering; the last drink did it. 'When d'yuh d'liver 'im?' he said thickly.

'If it's a deal – *right now!'*

He shoved out his hand. 'It's a deal!'

I nodded to my assistant to watch both ends, noted the time – 2300 – started to duck through the gate under the bar – when the juke box blared out: 'I'm My Own Granpaw!' The serviceman had orders to load it with old Americana and classics because I couldn't stomach the 'music' of 1970, but I hadn't known that tape was in it. I called out, 'Shut that off! Give the customer his money back.' I added, 'Storeroom, back in a moment,' and headed there with my Unmarried Mother following.

It was down the passage across from the johns, a steel door to which no one but my day manager and myself had a key; inside was a door to an inner room to which only I had a key. We went there.

He looked blearily around at the windowless walls. 'Where is 'e?'

'Right away.' I opened a case, the only thing in the room; it was a U.S.F.F. Co-ordinates Transformer Field Kit, series 1992, Mod. II – a beauty, no moving parts, weight twenty-three kilos fully charged, and shaped to pass as a suitcase. I had adjusted it precisely earlier that day; all I had to do was to shake out the metal net which limits the transformation field.

Which I did. 'Wha's that?' he demanded.

'Time machine,' I said and tossed the net over us.

'Hey!' he yelled and stepped back. There is a technique to this; the net has to be thrown so that the subject will instinctively step back *on to* the metal mesh, then you close the net with both of you inside completely – else you might leave shoe soles behind or a piece of foot, or scoop up a slice of floor. But that's all the skill it takes. Some agents con a subject into the net; I tell the truth and use that instant of utter astonishment to flip the switch. Which I did.

1030-V-3 April 1963-Cleveland, Ohio-Apex Bldg: 'Hey!' he repeated. 'Take this damn thing off!'

'Sorry,' I apologized and did so, stuffed the net into the case, closed it. 'You said you wanted to find him.'

'But – You said that was a time machine!'

I pointed out of a window. 'Does that look like November? Or New York?' While he was gawking at new buds

145

and spring weather, I reopened the case, took out a packet of hundred-dollar bills, checked that the numbers and signatures were compatible with 1963. The Temporal Bureau doesn't care how much you spend (it costs nothing) but they don't like unnecessary anachronisms. Too many mistakes and a general courtmartial will exile you for a year in a nasty period, say 1974 with its strict rationing and forced labour. I never make such mistakes, the money was okay. He turned around and said. 'What happened?'

'He's here. Go outside and take him. Here's expense money.' I shoved it at him and added, 'Settle him, then I'll pick you up.'

Hundred-dollar bills have a hypnotic effect on a person not used to them. He was thumbing them unbelievingly as I eased him into the hall, locked him out. The next jump was easy, a small shift in era.

1700-V-10 March 1964-Cleveland-Apex Bldg: There was a notice under the door saying that my lease expired next week; otherwise the room looked as it had a moment before. Outside, trees were bare and snow threatened; I hurried, stopping only for contemporary money and a coat, hat, and topcoat I had left there when I leased the room. I hired a car, went to the hospital. It took twenty minutes to bore the nursery attendant to the point where I could swipe the baby without being noticed; we went back to the Apex Building. This dial setting was more involved as the building did not yet exist in 1945. But I had precalculated it.

0100-V-20 Sept 1945-Cleveland-Skyview Motel: Field kit, baby, and I arrived in a motel outside town. Earlier I had registered as 'Gregory Johnson, Warren, Ohio', so we arrived in a room with curtains closed, windows locked, and doors bolted, and the floor cleared to allow for waver as the machine hunts. You can get a nasty bruise from a chair where it shouldn't be – not the chair of course, but backlash from the field.

No trouble. Jane was sleeping soundly; I carried her out, put her in a grocery box on the seat of a car I had provided earlier, drove to the orphanage, put her on the steps, drove two blocks to a 'service station' (the petroleum products sort) and phoned the orphanage, drove back in time to see them taking the box inside, kept going and abandoned the car near the motel – walked to it and jumped forward to the Apex Building in 1963.

2200-V-24 April 1963-Cleveland-Apex Bldg: I had cut the time rather fine – temporal accuracy depends on span, except on return to zero. If I had it right, Jane was discovering, out in the park this balmy spring night, that she wasn't quite as 'nice' a girl as she had thought. I grabbed a taxi to the home of those skinflints, had the hackie wait around a corner while I lurked in shadows.

Presently I spotted them down the street, arms around each other. He took her up on the porch and made a long job of kissing her good night – longer than I had thought. Then she went in and he came down the walk, turned away. I slid into step and hooked an arm in his. 'That's all, son,' I announced quietly. 'I'm back to pick you up.'

'*You!*' He gasped and caught his breath.

'Me. Now you know who *he* is – and after you think it over you'll know who *you* are ... and if you think hard enough, you'll figure out who the baby is ... and who *I* am.'

He didn't answer, he was badly shaken. It's a shock to have it proved to you that you can't resist seducing yourself. I took him to the Apex Building and we jumped again.

2300-VII-12 Aug 1985-Sub Rockies Base: I woke the duty sergeant, showed my I.D., told the sergeant to bed him down with a happy pill and recruit him in the morning. The sergeant looked sour but rank is rank, regardless of era; he did what I said – thinking, no doubt, that the next time we met he might be the colonel and I the sergeant. Which can happen in our corps. 'What name?' he asked.

I wrote it out. He raised his eyebrows. 'Like so, eh? *Hmm* —'

'You just do your job, Sergeant.' I turned to my companion. 'Son, your troubles are over. You're about to start the best job a man ever held – and you'll do well. I *know*.'

'But —'

' "But" nothing. Get a night's sleep, then look over the

147

proposition. You'll like it.'

'That you will!' agreed the sergeant. 'Look at me – born in 1917 – still around, still young, still enjoying life.' I went back to the jump-room, set everything on preselected zero.

2301-V-7 Nov 1970 NYC-'Pop's Place': I came out of the storeroom carrying a fifth of Drambuie to account for the minute I had been gone. My assistant was arguing with the customer who had been playing 'I'm My Own Granpaw!' I said, 'Oh, let him play it, then unplug it.' I was very tired.

It's rough, but somebody must do it and it's very hard to recruit anyone in the later years, since the Mistake of 1972. Can you think of a better source than to pick people all fouled up where they are and give them well-paid, interesting (even though dangerous) work in a necessary cause? Everybody knows now why the Fizzle War of 1963 fizzled. The Bomb with New York's number on it didn't go off, a hundred other things didn't go as planned – all arranged by the likes of me.

But not the Mistake of '72; that one is not our fault – and can't be undone; there's no paradox to resolve. A thing either is, or it isn't, now and for ever amen. But there won't be another like it; an order dated '1992' takes precedence any year.

I closed five minutes early, leaving a letter in the cash register telling my day manager that I was accepting his offer, so see my lawyer as I was leaving on a long vacation. The Bureau might or might not pick up his payments, but they want things left tidy. I went to the room back of the storeroom and forward to 1993.

2200-VII-12 Jan 1993-Sub Rockies Annex-HQ Temporal DOL: I checked in with the duty officer and went to my quarters, intending to sleep for a week. I had fetched the bottle we bet (after all, I won it) and took a drink before I wrote my report. It tasted foul and I wondered why I had ever liked Old Underwear. But it was better than nothing; I don't like to be cold sober, I think too much. But I don't really hit the bottle either; other people have snakes – *I* have people.

I dictated my report: forty recruitments all okayed by the Psych Bureau – counting my own, which I knew would be okayed. I was here, wasn't I? Then I taped a request for assignment to operations; I was sick of recruiting. I dropped both in the slot and headed for bed.

My eye fell on 'The By-Laws of Time', over my bed:

Never Do Yesterday What Should Be Done Tomorrow.
If At Last You Do Succeed, Never Try Again.
A Stitch in Time Saves Nine Billion.
A Paradox May be Paradoctored.
It is Earlier When You Think.
Ancestors Are Just People.
Even Jove Nods.

They didn't inspire me the way they had when I was a recruit; thirty subjective-years of time-jumping wears you down. I undressed and when I got down to the hide I looked at my belly. A Caesarian leaves a big scar but I'm so hairy now that I don't notice it unless I look for it.

Then I glanced at the ring on my finger.

The Snake That Eats Its Own Tail. Forever and Ever ... I *know* where *I* came from – but *where did all you zombies come from*?

I felt a headache coming on, but a headache powder is one thing I do not take. I did once – and you all went away.

So I crawled into bed and whistled out the light.

You aren't really there at all. There isn't anybody but me – Jane – here alone in the dark.

I miss you dreadfully!

THE SCIENCE FICTION BOOKS
OF ROBERT ANSON HEINLEIN

THE books are listed in chronological order of publication. The publisher of the first World edition is given, and where this was an American edition this is indicated by (US). Following this, all British editions are listed.

Short stories are indicated by 'collection', Omnibus Editions have a list of contents and these are cross-indexed by the use of In: references. All reissues of a book under a different title are listed with the original title.

Books published in hardcover are indicated by (hd) while all others are paperbacks. The date for each edition is also given. An asterisk (*) indicates that the edition was in print when this list was revised in 1976.

BIBLIOGRAPHY

ROCKET SHIP GALILEO
    Scribner (US hd), 1947; New English Library, 1971*.
SPACE CADET
    Scribner (US hd), 1948; Gollancz (hd), 1966*; New English Library, 1971*.
BEYOND THIS HORIZON
    Fantasy Press (US hd), 1948; Panther, 1967*.
    In: *The Robert Heinlein Omnibus*, 1966.
RED PLANET
    Scribner (US hd) 1949; Gollancz (hd), 1963*; Pan, 1967.
SIXTH COLUMN
    Gnome Press (US hd), 1949.
    Title change: *The Day After Tomorrow*.
        Signet (US), 1951; Mayflower, 1962; New English Library, 1972*.
WALDO and MAGIC INC. (collection)
    Doubleday (US hd), 1950; Pan, 1969*.
    In: *Three by Heinlein*, 1965.

Title change: *Waldo: Genius in Orbit*.
Avon (US), 1958.

THE MAN WHO SOLD THE MOON (collection)
Shasta Publishers (US hd), 1950; Sidgwick & Jackson (hd), 1950; Pan, 1955; New English Library, 1970*.
In: *The Robert Heinlein Omnibus*, 1958 & 1966 and *The Past Through Tomorrow*, 1967.

FARMER IN THE SKY
Scribner (US hd), 1950; Gollancz (hd), 1962*; Pan, 1967.

BETWEEN PLANETS
Scribner (US hd), 1951; Gollancz (hd), 1968*; New English Library, 1971*.

THE GREEN HILLS OF EARTH (collection)
Shasta Publishers (US hd), 1951; Sidgwick & Jackson (hd), 1954; Pan, 1956; Digit, 1962.
In: *The Robert Heinlein Omnibus*, 1958 & 1966 and *The Past Through Tomorrow*, 1966.

UNIVERSE
Dell (US), 1951.
Title change: expanded as *Orphans of the Sky*.
Gollancz (hd),1964*; Science Fiction Book Club (hd), 1964; Mayflower, 1965; Panther, 1975*.

THE PUPPET MASTERS
Doubleday (US hd), 1951; Museum Press (hd), 1953; Panther, 1960; Pan, 1969.
In: *Three by Heinlein*, 1965.

TOMORROW THE STARS (anthology edited by Robert Heinlein)
Doubleday (US hd), 1951.

THE ROLLING STONES
Scribner (US hd), 1952.
Title change: *Space Family Stone*.
Gollancz (hd), 1969*; New English Library, 1971*.

STARMAN JONES
Scribner (US hd), 1953; Sidgwick & Jackson (hd), 1954; Puffin (Penguin), 1966; Gollancz (hd), 1971*.

REVOLT IN 2100 (collection)
Shasta Publishers (US hd), 1953; Digit, 1959; Gollancz (hd), 1964; Science Fiction Book Club (hd), 1965; Pan, 1966; New English Library, 1971*.
In: *The Past Through Tomorrow*, 1966.

ASSIGNMENT IN ETERNITY (collection)
  Fantasy Press (US hd), 1953; Museum Press (hd), 1955;
    Digit, 1960; New English Library, 1971*.
THE STAR BEAST
  Scribner (US hd), 1954; New English Library, 1971*.
TUNNEL IN THE SKY
  Scribner (US hd), 1955; Gollancz (hd), 1965*; Pan, 1968.
DOUBLE STAR
  Doubleday (US hd), 1956; Michael Joseph (hd), 1958;
    Science Fiction Book Club (hd), 1959; Panther, 1960*.
TIME FOR THE STARS
  Scribner (US hd), 1956; Gollancz (hd), 1963*; Pan, 1968.
THE DOOR INTO SUMMER
  Doubleday (US hd), 1957; Panther, 1960; Gollancz (hd),
    1967*; Pan, 1970.
CITIZEN OF THE GALAXY
  Scribner (US hd), 1957; Gollancz (hd), 1969*; Puffin
    (Penguin), 1972*.
METHUSELAH'S CHILDREN
  Gnome Press (US hd), 1958; Gollancz (hd), 1963*; Science
    Fiction Book Club (hd), 1964; Pan, 1966; New English
    Library, 1971*.
  In: The Past Through Tomorrow, 1966.
HAVE SPACE SUIT – WILL TRAVEL
  Scribner (US hd), 1958; Gollancz (hd), 1970*; New Eng-
    lish Library, 1971*.
THE ROBERT HEINLEIN OMNIBUS (collection)
  Science Fiction Book Club (hd), 1958.
  Contains: The Green Hills of Earth and The Man Who
    Sold The Moon.
STARSHIP TROOPERS
  Putnam (US hd), 1959; New English Library, 1961*; New
    English Library (hd), 1975*.
THE UNPLEASANT PROFESSION OF JONATHAN HOAG (collec-
  tion)
  Gnome Press (US hd), 1960; Dobson (hd), 1964; Science
    Fiction Book Club (hd), 1965; Penguin, 1966; New
    English Library, 1976*.
  Title change: 6 × H
    Pyramid (US), 1962.
THE MENACE FROM EARTH (collection)
  Gnome Press (US hd), 1960; Dobson (hd), 1966*; Corgi,
    1968.

LOST LEGACY (collection)
Digit, 1960
STRANGER IN A STRANGE LAND
Putnam (US hd), 1961; New English Library, 1965*; New
English Library (hd), 1975*.
PODKAYNE OF MARS
Putnam (US hd), 1963; New English Library, 1969*.
GLORY ROAD
Putnam (US hd), 1963; New English Library, 1965*; New
English Library (hd), 1976*.
FARNHAM'S FREEHOLD
Putnam (US hd), 1965; Dobson (hd), 1965; Corgi, 1967.
THREE BY HEINLEIN (collection)
Doubleday (US hd), 1965.
Title change: *A Heinlein Triad.*
Gollancz (hd), 1966.
Contains: *The Puppet Masters, Waldo* and *Magic Inc.*
THE MOON IS A HARSH MISTRESS
Putnam (US hd), 1966; Dobson (hd), 1967; New English
Library. 1969*.
THE ROBERT HEINLEIN OMNIBUS (collection)
Sidgwick & Jackson (hd), 1966.
Contains: *Beyond This Horizon, The Green Hills of
Earth* and *The Man Who Sold the Moon.*
THE WORLDS OF ROBERT A. HEINLEIN (collection)
Ace (US), 1966; New English Library, 1970*.
THE PAST THROUGH TOMORROW (collection)
Putnam (US hd), 1967.
Contains: *The Man Who Sold the Moon, The Green
Hills of Earth, Revolt In 2100* and *Methuselah's Chil-
dren.*
I WILL FEAR NO EVIL
Putnam (US hd), 1970; New English Library (hd), 1971*;
New English Library, 1972*.
TIME ENOUGH FOR LOVE
Putnam (US hd), 1973; New English Library (hd), 1974;
New English Library, 1975*.
THE BEST OF ROBERT HEINLEIN (collection edited by Angus
Wells)
Sphere, 1973; Sidgwick & Jackson (hd), 1973*.
The Best of Robert Heinlein: 1939–1942. Sphere, 1975*.
The Best of Robert Heinlein: 1947–1959. Sphere, 1977*.

More superlative Science Fiction
from Sphere

THE BEST OF ARTHUR C CLARKE: 1937–1971

The author of the world-famous *2001: A SPACE
ODYSSEY* is concerned with both the scientific and the
metaphysical aspect of science fiction. A founder member of
the British Interplanetary Society, Clarke originated the
proposal for the use of satellites in communications. The
eighteen stories in this collection have been selected to show
Clarke's development both as a scientist and as an
imaginative writer, and include *THE SENTINEL*, the
original story upon which the screenplay for *2001* was based.

CONTENTS:

Travel by Wire/Retreat from Earth/The Awakening/
Whacky/Castaway/History Lesson/Hide and Seek/Second
Dawn/The Sentinel/The Star/Refugee/Venture to the
Moon/Into the Comet/Summertime on Icarus/Death and
the Senator/Hate/Sunjammer/A Meeting with Medusa.

With a bibliography and an introduction by the author.

0 7221 2437 6   65p

THE BEST OF FRANK HERBERT: 1952–1964

Frank Herbert is justly regarded as one of the giants of science fiction, most famous for his classic novel *DUNE*. He brings to his writing, together with a vivid imagination, a fundamental optimism that makes him one of the most enjoyable writers in the field. As he says in his own introduction to this collection:

'. . . science fiction strives to translate our old dreams into new ones, and, in the process, to make the nightmares less fearsome.'

The development of his talent is demonstrated in this selection from his earlier writing.

CONTENTS:

Looking for Something/Nightmare Blues/Dragon in the Sea/Cease Fire/Egg and Ashes/Marie Celeste Move.

With a bibliography and an introduction by the author.

0 7221 4523 3   55p

THE BEST OF FRITZ LEIBER

'I write my stories against backgrounds of science, history, fantasy world of swords and sorcery, the intensely strange everyday human mind, and the weird and occult, about which I am a skeptic, yet which interest me vastly.'

Thus Fritz Leiber introduces his unique and superbly readable blend of fantasy and science fiction, amply represented in this collection of his stories. Fritz Leiber is the holder of both Hugo and Nebula awards.

CONTENTS:

Sanity/Wanted – an Enemy/The Man Who Never Grew Young/The Ship Sails at Midnight/The Enchanted Forest/Coming Attraction/Poor Superman/A Pail of Air/The Foxholes of Mars/The Big Holiday/The Night He Cried/The Big Trek/Space-Time for Springers/Try and Change the Past/A Deskful of Girls/Rump-Titty-Titty-Tum-Tah-Tee/Little Old Miss Macbeth/Mariana/The Man Who Made Friends with Electricity/The Good New Days/Gonna Roll the Bones/America the Beautiful.

With a bibliography and an introduction by the author.

0 7221 5474 7   60p

THE BEST OF CLIFFORD D SIMAK

Clifford D Simak wins science fiction awards with the regularity of a brilliant film director winning Oscars. In 1952 he won the International Fantasy Award with his novel *CITY*. In 1958 his novelette *THE BIG FRONT YARD* won the Hugo Award, which he won again in 1964 with his novel *WAY STATION*. Simak's talent lies in his use of 'ordinary', good people, saints rather than sinners, allied to his marvellous ability to weave a story that fascinates, intrigues and excites. The ten stories in this collection illustrate the development of this pastoral and most compassionate of science fiction writers.

CONTENTS:

Madness from Mars / Sunspot Purge / The Sitters / A Death in the House / Final Gentleman / Shotgun Cure / Day of Truce / Small Deer / The Thing in the Stone / The Autumn Land.

With a bibliography and an introduction by the author.

0 7221 7836 0   60p

THE BEST OF A E VAN VOGT

A E Van Vogt is one of the classic names in science fiction, and one of the genre's most influential and widely-read authors since the 1940s. His novels, *SLAN*, *THE WEAPON SHOPS OF ISHER*, *THE WORLD OF NULL-A* and *THE PAWNS OF NULL-A* are rightly regarded as milestones in science fiction literature. His short stories, a representative collection of which appear in this book, are equally impressive.

CONTENTS:

Vault of the Beast/The Weapon Shop/The Storm/Juggernaut/Hand of the Gods/The Cataaaaa/The Monster/Dear Pen Pal/The Green Forest/War of Nerves/The Expendables/Silkies in Space/The Proxy Intelligence.

With a bibliography and an introduction by the author.

0 7221 8774 2   60p